John Sargent

The Mine, a Dramatic Poem

To which Are Added Two Historic Odes. Third Edition

John Sargent

The Mine, a Dramatic Poem
To which Are Added Two Historic Odes. Third Edition

ISBN/EAN: 9783744716116

Printed in Europe, USA, Canada, Australia, Japan

Cover: Foto ©Andreas Hilbeck / pixelio.de

More available books at **www.hansebooks.com**

Published as the Act directs by T. Cadell, Strand, Feb.ʸ 11. 1788.

THE
MINE:

A

DRAMATIC POEM.

TO WHICH ARE ADDED

TWO HISTORIC ODES.

By JOHN SARGENT, Esq.

THE THIRD EDITION.

LONDON:

PRINTED FOR T. CADELL, JUN. AND W. DAVIES,
(SUCCESSORS TO MR. CADELL) STRAND.

1796.

THE

M I N E:

A

DRAMATIC POEM.

―――――――

Ευφαμεῖτε δε· χαρεῖτε
Γᾶς ὑπο κευθεσιν αγυγίοισι.

ÆSCHYLUS.

Approach!—great Nature studiously behold,
And eye the Mine without a wish for Gold.

POPE.

PREFACE.

As it is often pleasing to the Reader to be made acquainted with the accidental origin of a Poem, I shall not dissemble that the following took its rise from a short paragraph which appeared in the public prints a few years ago. The purport of it was, that a nobleman of great rank at Vienna had been condemned to the mines; and that his wife, a lady of high extraction, and in the bloom of youth and beauty, had taken the desperate resolution of sharing his fate, and of accompanying him to those abodes of wretchedness. A fimilar circumftance, I find, is related in fome letters written by Mr. Everard, an Italian, a tranflation of which is inferted in the tenth volume of the Annual Regifter. They contain an adventure, of which he was witnefs, at the quickfilver mine at Idria in Friuli; and as they exprefs in a natural and lively manner the feelings that muft arife in every humane breaft upon fuch an occafion, I fhall take the liberty to tranfcribe them.

LETTER I.

DEAR SIR,

THE pleafure I always take in writing to you, wherever I am, and whatever

doing, in fome meafure difpels my prefent
uneafinefs; an uneafinefs caufed at once
by the difagreeable afpeĉt of every thing
round me, and by the more difagreeable
circumftances of the Count Alberti, with
whom you were once acquainted. You
remember him one of the gayeft, moft
agreeable perfons at the court of Vienna;
at once the example of the men, and the
favourite of the fair fex. I often heard
you repeat his name with efteem, as one
of the few that did honour to the prefent
age; as poffeffed of generofity and pity in
the higheft degree; as one who made no
other ufe of fortune, but to alleviate the
diftreffes of mankind. That gentleman,
Sir, I wifh I could fay is now no more;
yet, too unhappily for him, he exifts, but

in a fituation more terrible than the moft gloomy imagination can conceive.

After paffing through feveral parts of the Alps, and having vifited Germany, I thought I could not well return home without vifiting the quickfilver mines at Idria, and feeing thofe dreadful fubterraneous caverns, where thoufands are condemned to refide, fhut out from all hopes of ever feeing the cheerful light of the fun, and obliged to toil out a miferable life under the whips of imperious tafkmafters. Imagine to yourfelf an hole in the fide of a mountain, of about five yards over; down this you are let in a kind of bucket, more than a hundred fathom, the profpect growing ftill more gloomy, yet ftill widening, as you defcend. At length, after swinging in terrible suspense for some time in this precarious situation, you at last reach the bottom, and tread on the ground; which, by its hollow found under your feet, and the reverberations of the echo, seems thundering at every step you take. In this gloomy and frightful solitude, you are enlightened by the feeble gleam of lamps, here and there disposed, so as that the wretched inhabitants of these mansions can go from one part to another without a guide. And yet let me assure you, that though they by custom could see objects very distinctly by those lights, I could scarce discern, for some time, any thing, not even the person who came with me to shew me these scenes of horror.

From this description, I suppose, you

have but a difagreeable idea of the place ;
yet let me affure you, that it is a palace, if
we compare the habitation with its inhabitants. Such wretches my eyes never beheld. The blacknefs of their vifages only
ferves to cover an horrid palenefs, caufed
by the noxious qualities of the mineral
they are employed in procuring. As they
in general confift of malefactors condemned for life to this tafk, they are fed
at the public expence ; but they feldom
confume much provifion, as they lofe their
appetites in a fhort time, and commonly
in about two years expire, from a total
contraction of all the joints of the body.

In this horrid manfion I walked after
my guide for fome time, pondering on
the ftrange tyranny and avarice of mankind, when I was accofted by a voice

behind me, calling me by name, and en-
quiring after my health with the moſt
cordial affection. I turned, and ſaw a
creature, all black and hideous, who ap-
proached me, and with a moſt piteous ac-
cent demanding, "Ah! Mr. Everard, don't
" you know me?" Good God! what was
my ſurpriſe, when through the veil of his
wretchedneſs I diſcovered the features of
my old and dear friend Alberti! I flew
to him with affection, and, after a tear
of condolence, aſked how he came there.
To this he replied, that having fought a
duel with a General of the Auſtrian in-
fantry, againſt the Emperor's command,
and having left him for dead, he was
obliged to fly into one of the foreſts of
Iſtria, where he was firſt taken, and afterwards ſheltered, by ſome banditti, who

had long infefted that quarter. With thefe he had lived for nine months, till, by a clofe inveftiture of the place in which they were concealed, and after a very obftinate refiftance, in which the greater part of them were killed, he was taken and carried to Vienna, in order to be broke alive upon the wheel. However, upon arriving at the capital, he was quickly known; and feveral of the affociates of his accufation and danger witneffing his innocence, his punifhment of the rack was changed into that of perpetual confinement and labour in the mines of Idria: a fentence, in my opinion, a thoufand times worfe than death.

As Alberti was giving me this account, a young woman came up to him, who at once I faw to be born for better fortune:

the dreadful fituation of the place was not able to deftroy her beauty; and even in this fcene of wretchednefs, fhe feemed to have charms to grace the moft brilliant affembly. This Lady was in fact daughter to one of the firft families of Germany; and having tried every means to procure her lover's pardon without effect, was at laft refolved to fhare his miferies, as fhe could not relieve them. With him fhe accordingly defcended into thefe manfions, from whence few of the living return; and with him fhe is contented to live, forgetting the gaieties of life; with him to toil, defpifing the fplendors of opulence, and contented with the confcioufnefs of her own conftancy.

I am, dear Sir,

Yours, &c.

LETTER II.

DEAR SIR,

MY laſt to you was expreſſive, and
perhaps too much ſo, of the gloomy ſituation of my mind. I own the deplorable
ſituation of the worthy man deſcribed in
it, was enough to add double ſeverity to
the hideous manſion. At preſent, however, I have the happineſs of informing
you, that I was ſpectator of the moſt affecting ſcene I ever yet beheld. Nine
days after I had written my laſt, a perſon
came poſt from Vienna to the little vil-
lage near the mouth of the greater ſhaft :
he was ſoon followed by a ſecond, and he
by a third. Their firſt enquiry was after
the unfortunate Count ; and I happening
to overhear the demand, gave them the

beſt information. Two of theſe were
the brother and couſin of the Lady; the
third was an intimate friend and fellow-
ſoldier to the Count : they came with his
pardon, which had been procured by the
General with whom the duel had been
fought, and who was perfectly recovered
from his wounds. I led them with all
the expedition of joy down to his dreary
abode, and preſented to him his friends;
and informed him of the happy change
in his circumſtances. It would be impoſſi-
ble to deſcribe the joy that brightened in
his grief-worn countenance; nor was the
young Lady's emotion leſs vivid at ſeeing
her friends, and hearing of her huſband's
freedom. Some hours were employed in
mending the appearance of this faithful
couple; nor could I without a tear behold

him taking leave of the former wretched companions of his toil. To one he left his mattock, to another his working clothes, to a third his little houſehold utenſils, ſuch as were neceſſary for him in that ſituation.* We ſoon emerged from the mine, when he once again reviſited the light of the ſun, that he had totally deſpaired of ever ſeeing. A poſt-chaiſe and four were ready the next morning to take them to Vienna ; where, I am ſince informed by a letter from himſelf, they are returned. The Empreſs has again taken him into favour ; his fortune and rank are reſtored ; and he and his fair part-ner now have the pleaſing ſatisfaction of feeling happineſs with double reliſh, as they once knew what it was to be miſerable.

I am, dear Sir,

Yours, &c.

TO this affecting detail of our Italian traveller, I shall subjoin a picture of the same kind, delineated by the hand of an eminent Greek historian. It is the more deserving notice, as it contains a curious account of the manner in which the gold mines were worked in the remotest ages; and as it may convince us, however we may pride ourselves upon our advancement in knowledge and refinement, that we still adopt the barbarous practices of unenlightened times, when, in spite of the dictates of humanity, and of a pure and benevolent religion, we persist to inflict upon our fellow-creatures a punishment so much worse than death *.

* It is but just to remark, that some of the principal European mines are not converted to these tyrannical

" On the confines of Egypt, Arabia, and Ethiopia," fays Diodorus Siculus, " there is a tract of land abounding with minerals, and particularly with gold, which is extracted with infinite labour and expence. The foil, which is hard and black, is interfected with veins of marble of the moft brilliant whitenefs and luftre. In this fpot the fuperintendants of the mines employ a great number of workmen to procure the ore ; for the kings of Egypt fend all thofe perfons to the mines who have been convicted of any crime, as well as the prifoners taken in war, and every one who,

purpofes. Thofe in the foreft of Hartz, which I have vifited with peculiar pleafure, are regulated by the moft admirable rules of humanity and found policy. A curious and pleafing account of that very fingular and induftrious community may be found in a work of Monf. de Luc, intitled, " Lettres fur la Terre," tom. iii. lett. 63 & 64.

being falfely or juftly accufed, has incur-
red their refentment. Their families are
often involved in the fame fate ; and their
fovereign, by thefe means, not only fatisfies
his vengeance, but derives a great advan-
tage from their punifhment. Thefe un-
happy perfons, the number of whom is
very confiderable, have chains faftened upon
their legs, and are condemned to toil day
and night without intermiffion, or any hope
of efcaping from their wretchednefs : for
they have foreign foldiers fet over them,
who fpeak a different language from themfelves, which renders it impoffible for
them to corrupt their guards, either by fa-
miliarity or promifes. When the foil which
contains the ore is too hard, they foften it
by fire ; after which they apply their ma-
nual exertions, and break it in pieces with

iron tools adapted to that purpofe. A fkil-
ful perfon fuperintends the bufinefs, who is
acquainted with the veins of the mine,
and directs the workmen to them. The
ftrongeft prifoners are employed to cleave
the rocks with fharp iron maliets; a work
which demands only bodily ftrength, and
no fuperior dexterity. They drive their
wedges obliquely, as they are directed by
the glimmering of the ore; and as it is
often neceffary to make fudden turns to
follow the veins of the mineral, and becaufe the fubterraneous cavities in which
they work are extremely dark, they have
lamps affixed to their foreheads. By varying their pofture as often as their fituation requires it, they break off the pieces
of rock, which fall down at their feet. In
this manner they toil inceffantly, being

compelled by the menaces and the ftripes of their tafk-mafters. Into the fmaller cavities of the rock little children are fent, who extract from thence the minute pieces of ore, and convey them to the mouth of the mine. The men of about thirty years of age have a certain quantity of the mineral given them, which they pound in mortars with iron peftles, and reduce to the fize of a grain of millet. The women and old men then receive it, and placing it under grind-ftones, which are ranged in order for that purpofe, they difpofe of themfelves two or three to each mill, and grind it till they have reduced it to the finenefs of meal, of which they have a fample given them. It is impoffible not to compaffionate the extreme mifery of thefe wretches, who are not permitted to be-

ftow any care on their perfons, nor to cover their nakednefs. No mercy is at any
time fhewn either to the fick or maimed,
to the weaknefs of the female fex, or the
debility of age ; but they are compelled by
ftripes to perfevere, till their ftrength is
exhaufted, and they expire with fatigue *.
Thus thefe unfortunate people have no hope
but in death, and the horrors of their fituation make them dread the prolongation of

* The fufferings of thofe who were condemned to this
exquifite punifhment, gave occafion, as Le Clerc conjectures, to the fictions of the ancients refpecting Hades,
or the fhades below.—According to tradition, he was
king of Epirus, in which country, we learn from Strabo,
that there were many mines. He was efteemed the God
of Riches on this account, and denominated Plutus ; and
was fuppofed alfo to prefide over the dead, becaufe few
who entered thofe fubterraneous abodes ever returned
from them. We find the young man in the Captives of
Plautus, who was juft returned from the ftone quarries,

life.—The fuperintendants, who take the
ore when it is reduced to a fine powder,
finifh their work in the following manner:
They fpread it upon planks a little in-
clined, and wafh it copioufly with water.
The earthy particles are thus carried away
by the force of the ftream, while the gold,
on account of its weight, is left behind.
This operation being frequently repeated,
they rub the ore lightly between their
hands; after which they dry it with fine
fponges, till all impurity is removed, and
the powder is perfeftly clean. Other work-

expreffing himfelf very feelingly on the occafion :—

  Vidi ego multa fæpe pifta quæ Acherunti fierent
  Cruciamenta, verum enimvero nulla adæque eft
    Acheruns
Atque ubi ego fui in lapicidinis.—Aft. v. f. 4.

      See LE CLERC's Note to the Theogony of
        Hefiod, p. 379, Robinfon's edit.

men then take it, and having weighed and
meafured it, put it into earthen pots. A
certain proportion of lead is afterwards
added to it, with a few grains of falt, a little
tin, and fome barley meal. They pour
the whole into covered veffels, exactly
luted, which they place in a furnace for
five days and nights fucceffively : then,
having allowed it time to cool, no further
mixture of impure matter is found, but the
gold is entirely purified, with very little
wafte. Such is the manner in which they
obtain gold on the confines of Egypt, with
immenfe labour. Thus Nature herfelf
points out with what great difficulty the
acquifition of this metal is attended ;
which, when procured, can only be retain-
ed by extreme caution and diligence ; and

the ufe of which is productive of fo much
delight and folicitude*!"

Such is the account of that humane
hiftorian. With refpect to the following
poem, I fhall only detain the reader by
one fhort reflection.

As the limits of true philofophy are ex-
tended, the writer of every fpecies of com-
pofition is entitled to avail himfelf of its

---

* Diodorus Siculus, lib. iii. p. 150. edit. Rhodomani.—It is probable the hiftorian was an eye-witnefs of
what he relates with fo much minutenefs, as he took
very extenfive journeys to collect materials for his work.
The reader who is defirous of knowing what analogy
there is between the ancient manner of working the gold
mines, and the procefs adopted at prefent, may compare
the above account with that of Don Antonio de Ulloa,
who defcribes the management of the mines of Caxa, in
the province of Quito.—Ulloa, vol. i. p. 450.

difcoveries, and by deriving new images and fimilitudes from them, to confer on his work a greater degree of utility and em-bellifhment. In an age when the ftudies of natural hiftory are profecuted with pecu-liar fuccefs, an attempt to unite poetry and fcience * may perhaps not be unfavourably received, or at leaft may be exempted from the charge either of affeƐtation or pedantry. It will occur to the candid, that the imagination, in fuch cafes, may

* " C'eft par la Poefie que l'Hiftoire Naturelle penetre jufques dans les cabinets de ceux qui ne prennent pas la peine de l'aller chercher dans les champs ou dans les abîmes de la terre. Lorfqu'une image nous a charmé dans un poeme, nous devenons curieux d'en voir la realité, et nous ne l'avons plutot vue que la memoire en conferve le fidele depot."—See a curious and mafterly Differtation of Profeffor Michaëlis, on the reciprocal In-fluence of Language and Opinion, p. 84, printed at Bre-men, 1762.——An Author of our own nation has

be indulged, without deferting truth ; and that whatever contributes to bring us acquainted with the works of Nature, has a tendency both to enlarge the underftanding, and to improve the heart.

pointed out, with great ingenuity, the beauties which many eminent poets have derived from this fource. May it not, however, juftly excite our furprife, that a writer of fo much fagacity and tafte fhould have profcribed any part of the various productions of Nature, by pronouncing " the mineral kingdom to be fteril, and unaccommodated to defcription ?"—Effay on the Poetical Ufe of Natural Hiftory, by Mr. Aikin, p. 33.

LAVINGTON,
JULY 30, 1784.

PERSONS *of the* DRAMA.

COUNT MAURICE,⎫ *Hungarian Noblemen.*
LEOPOLD,　　　　⎭

CONRAD,　　⎫
FREDERIC,　⎬ *Prisoners in the Mine.*
JULIANA,　　⎭

GNOMES *and* SUBTERRANEOUS SPIRITS.

SCENE,

The Quicksilver Mine at IDRIA *.

---

* The Stage, whenever the Gnomes enter, is to be suddenly illuminated, but at other times is to be kept as dark as possible.

THE

M I N E.

COUNT MAURICE, LEOPOLD.

COUNT MAURICE.

OUR short allotted interval of rest
From yon faint noise, I deem, is almost spent;
For through this subterraneous prison-house
The fragrant breath of Heaven hath never blown;
Nor know we the sweet interchange of day
And balmy night: we to laborious tasks
Arise, but thou to liberty and life.

LEOPOLD.

Yet without thee, whose generous aid sustain'd
My fainting spirit, how shall I revisit
The day-spring, how accept the proffer'd boon
Of long-wish'd freedom?

COUNT MAURICE.
              'Tis three months and more,
Since on this pendent vault, with trembling hand,
I etch'd the fad memorial of my name,
And on its fparry architrave began
To chronicle each day of growing woe;
Yet innocence, and Heaven's kind difpenfation
To the deep fuffering of my defperate wrongs,
So reconcile me, that with this hard yoke
I quarrel not, but in my friend's releafe
A higher argument of comfort find,
Than forrow in my endlefs fervitude.

LEOPOLD.
  O wondrous virtue!

COUNT MAURICE.
              What a fate was ours!
Aufpicious fortune fmil'd upon our birth,
Shower'd on our profperous head each lavifh gift
Of noblenefs and power, e'en with the bounty
Of a fond parent; then with envious guile,

Like a harſh ſtep-dame, tore her boons away,
Made the meek nature of our Sovereign change
To bittereſt cruelty, and turn'd our merit
Of loyal ſervice to opprobrious guilt.

LEOPOLD.

Was it for this, when faithleſs kings combin'd,
And in her youthful hand the ſceptre ſhook—
When each ſad hour was fruitful with the tidings
Of ſome new loſs—was it for this we ſummon'd
Our vaſſals to the field, brav'd every peril,
And made her boldly face a world in arms?

COUNT MAURICE.

Yes, I remember when in Preſburg's walls
She ſought her brave Hungarians[1]; in her arms
The infant prince ſhe claſp'd, who to her neck
Clung trembling at the dazzling files, and ſound
Of martial minſtrelſy: " Defend," ſhe cried,
" Your Queen, with foes beſet ; her Son proteƈt,
" And ſave the guardian of your laws and realm."

LEOPOLD.

What loyalty, what ardent valour beam'd
In every eye! Yet, the rough conflict paſt,
Our worthieſt deeds were loſt, our love miſconſtrued
To factious pride, and patriot zeal requited
With theſe diſaſtrous ſhades and penal chains.

COUNT MAURICE.

Had we o'erleap'd each bound and high reſtraint
Of ſacred duty—againſt the throne itſelf
Rais'd traiterous war—what elſe had we deſerv'd
Than to be pent within theſe diſmal tracts
Of darkneſs and affliction? to behold
Sights of infernal toil and horrid woe?
Our birth and noble natures to forget,
And mixing with a baſe promiſcuous crew,
To ſhare the drudgery of their ſervile taſks?
But thy glad hour of freedom comes, and half
My ſufferings end.

LEOPOLD.

　　　　　　　What boots it that the body
Be freed from harſh reſtraint, if tyrannous grief

Inthrall the mind? I will not, cannot leave thee!

COUNT MAURICE.

Spurn not thy Sovereign's mercy. Wouldſt thou
    make

My miſery more perfeᶜt?

LEOPOLD.

            No, I would dwell

For years contented in this vaporous dungeon,

Delve the thick-ribbed rocks with fervent toil,

And hear the viewleſs winds inceſſant roar,

Impriſon'd like ourſelves within the depths

Of theſe perplexed labyrinths—could I ſhare

Thy woes, and ranſom our remaining age.

COUNT MAURICE.

  Go, and may Heaven its own high purpoſes

Ordain! Whate'er my portion, I exult

In thy deliverance: when thou ſhalt inhale

The breezy air, and with a thirſt as keen

As the parch'd Arab feels on Nubia's ſand,

Drink the refreſhing ſtream of living light—
Thy ſoul-felt ecſtacy ſhall I partake
'Midſt this abhorr'd privation.   But I'm ſummon'd
To ignominious toil.—Farewell for ever ! [*Exeunt.*

Enter ² GNOMES *and* SUBTERRANEOUS
SPIRITS.

   To us our Queen, who in the central earth,
'Midſt fiery lavas, on baſaltine ſeas
Deep-thron'd, the illimitable waſte enjoys,
Enormous ſolitude ! has given theſe
Her ſubterraneous realms ; bids us dwell here
In the abyſs of darkneſs, and exert
Immortal Alchymy ; the criſped founts
To cryſtallize, and point the gliſtening ſpar,
Ruby and hyacinth, and precious ore,
Quickening fell Avarice, and obdurate Pride.
Yet want we not ſuch pleaſures as befit
Celeſtial minds : for in this boundleſs gulf,
When man, to whom a doleful priſon it ſeems,

Would wreak on Innocence fome foul revenge,

Her fainting virtue we fuftain, and waft

Her agonizing fighs to Mercy's ear.

But fee! our Queen approaches.

QUEEN *of the* GNOMES, SUBTERRANEOUS
SPIRITS.

QUEEN.

Ye Gnomes, ye puiffant Spirits, who delight

To range th' unfathomable depths of night;

Who thefe ftupendous realms undaunted fway,

To whom this cold is heat, this darknefs day;

Speed thro' the earthy layers your fluid courfe,

Loofe the foft fand, the marle obftructive force;

Of latent rills the bubbling fount unlock,

And gem with cryftal every gliftening rock;

Each devious cleft, each fecret cell explore,

And from its fiffures draw the ductile ore;

Thro' ponderous fhades diffufe the golden rays,

And bid th' imperial Lord of Metals blaze [3];

His radiant form invest with many a zone [4],

And place the tyrant on Peruvia's throne.

From trickling drops distil the silvery dew,

Pale as the crescent's be its virgin hue:

The starry lustre let Platina share,

While wondering Dian hails her argent pair [5]:

To these the deadly grain of Saturn join,

And Cytherea's favourite ore combine [6];

Let each soft tint the beauteous mass pervade,

And vivid lights contrast with ambient shade.

'Midst flinty crags, on bed of glittering spars,

Spread the red Mineral of indignant Mars:

Tho' fierce, he rushes to the Magnet's side,

And as an ardent bridegroom clasps his bride:

To his dark caves the Naiads lead by stealth,

And let Hygeia boast her liquid wealth [7].

Quick as thro' night electric eddies gleam,

Or atoms quiver in the solar beam,

Make the bright orbs of volant Hermes shine,

And every charm reflect from Beauty's shrine [8].

Go too, ye minifters of wrath and pain,
Awake the horrors of our drear domain,
That ftartling mortals may confefs your might,
And own the wonders work'd in tenfold night:
In mineral cells the fecret damp prepare,
Sublime each fume, and fix the poifonous air;
Of hoary fens exalt the ftagnant breath,
And load the paffing gale with plagues and death [9].
Thro' yelling gulfs outrageous whirlwinds urge [10],
Or curl the toffing pool with fiery furge [11];
Bid flaming cataracts round Vefuvius glow,
Bid Hecla thunder thro' incumbent fnow;
From Cotopaxi's heights the deluge pour,
And melt a thoufand winters' frozen ftore [12];
Beneath the main expanfive vapours raife,
And with metallic embers feed the blaze,
Till the black vortex of the water boils,
And Ocean wonders at his new-form'd ifles [13];
Or riven mountains from their bafe are hurl'd [14],
And elemental wars convulfe the world.

Such be your tafks to day: a chofen band

Within the precinĉts of this echoing mine

With me remain, to fuccour a fad pair

Whom the harfh mandate of misjudging rule,

And fuborn'd violence, here conftrain to dwell.

Now to your works.

The GNOMES *divide and fing.*

Sylphs, no more in haunted groves

Boaft your vegetable loves;

Nor the bloom young Zephyrs fling

O'er the vermil cheek of Spring;

Nor the dewy fragrance, born

From the treffes of the morn.

Wherefoe'er our footfteps turn,

Rubies blufh, and diamonds burn;

Every grot and filver cave

Streams of milk and amber lave [15];

And our bow'rs such perfumes give,

As mortals cannot taste and live [16];

From controuling seasons free,

We labour our high alchymy,

Nor borrow from the garish day

One beam, to light us on our way;

But beneath the Atlantic flood

Wind our subterraneous road:

Our torch the phosporus, our car

The jacinth, or the emerald spar,

Wondrous toils we here pursue,

Never ending, always new;

Blending, in our vast retreat,

Moist and dry, and cold and heat;

Till our skill prolific tries

All Nature's contrarieties.

QUEEN.

No more—from yonder arch some mournful step

And plaintive sighs I hear. 'Tis Juliana;

Guide her, ye faithful Gnomes, left her foft foot
Againft the fharp flint prefs : and from her head
Brufh every noxious vapour.   Hark! fhe ftrives
To wake the echoes of this lonefome cave :
We will retire and liften.

Exeunt the GNOMES, with their QUEEN.

JULIANA fings.
Ye grots and midnight fhade,
By toiling mifery vocal made,
Thro' your abhorr'd fojourn I cheerful rove;
Each fcene of youth and pleafure fled,
Tho' to the world my heart be dead,
Still let it live to innocence and love,

JULIANA, FREDERIC.

FREDERIC.
How does that fweet and lenient cadence differ
From the fierce parley and uproar, that rend
Thefe rocks and hideous caverns!

JULIANA.

Now the hour

Of tafk is nigh, and from their flinty pallets

The wretched inmates crawl, with haggard mien

Aduft, and unftrung arms unfit to wield

Their maffy implements: tho' I have look'd

Whole days upon this fcene of various woe,

Still when the mournful din and murmur fwell,

It ftrikes me to the quick.—But fure I fee

The hoary prifoner, whofe confiderate kindnefs

Has challeng'd my regard; through him perchance

I may refolve my doubts.—Thou good old man,

Though bow'd with age and toil, who ftill art cheerful,

Would that the meffenger of joyful tidings,

Who came laft night, had fpoke thy glad releafe!

Know'ft thou for whom he brought the happy news?

FREDERIC.

To Leopold he came; but the poor Count,

Though to his friend, they fay, he bade farewell

With tears of gladneſs and with heart-felt rapture,

Now pines with double anguiſh.

JULIANA.

Where—where is he ?

Say, doſt thou ſee him at his wonted ſtation ?

FREDERIC.

Scarce can I pierce the air with labouring eye,

Such pitchy darkneſs reigns ; yet near yon rock,

Where drops the lingering ſtream, a form I ſee,

That reſts incumbent on a wrenching mattock,

And ſeems entranc'd in melancholy thought.

JULIANA.

Alas ! 'tis he. Oh ! what a dreadful change

Has that mean garb, and the corroſive air,

Work'd on his youthful form !

FREDERIC.

Thy boſom melts,

As for a friend, with agonizing pity :

Why art thou mov'd ſo deeply?

a form I see,
That rests incumbent on a wrenching mattock,
And seems entranc'd in melancholy thought.

Published as the Act directs by T. Cadell Strand Feb.r 11 1786.

JULIANA.

I have heard
The unexampled torments he endur'd,
And the bold ardor of his steady soul:
When brib'd by his insidious foes with promise
Of pardon and of wealth, would he accuse
His innocent friend, he scorn'd the base proposal,
And nobly chose with Leopold to suffer.

FREDERIC.

And the fair partner of his soul, if fame
Report the truth, confirm'd his generous purpose;
And, tho' of transient bliss she scarce had tasted
A few short moments, tore the bands asunder,
And to her love and life preferr'd his honour.

JULIANA.

How pure was her affection!

FREDERIC.

The sad thought
Calls from thine eyes, I see, the starting tears,
That silent fall beneath thy mantling veil.

Pardon, fair ſtranger, if thy ſorrows move

The curious pity of a wretch, who long

Has known this dread abode : tho' I have toil'd

For many a diſmal year, ne'er have I ſeen

A form like thine, ſo delicate and tender,

That, as an heavenly apparition, glides

Amidſt the ſhades of night.   What ſtrange deſign

Of ardent friendſhip, or romantic courage,

Led thee this peſtilential air to breathe ?

How couldſt thou ever gain admittance here ?

JULIANA.
Vain was each effort ; but relenting fortune

Look'd down at laſt, and proſper'd all my wiſhes :

Oft the ſtern guard refus'd, till ſoft intreaties,

And gold well-miniſter'd, bent to my purpoſe

His rugged ſoul.—But ſpare thy kind inquiries :

O queſtion me no more !

FREDERIC.
                    If fear or anguiſh

Urge thee to hide thy ſad myſterious errand,

Yet deign my friendly counfel to accept ;
For little doft thou know what perils dire
Thou muft encounter here, 'midft chilling night
And poifonous mineral fumes.—Hark ! how the horn,
With fhrill notes echoing round the vaulted rocks,
Proclaims the hour of toil.   Now to our tafks
We go, with infult driven, and goading ftripes.

JULIANA.

Oh worfe than burthen'd beafts ! they only feel
Immediate pain ; while your more fuffering minds
'Midft prefent anguifh image paft delight,
And all the hopelefs future.

FREDERIC.
                              Ere I leave thee,
Let me unfold my fears, left aught thou fuffer
From bold incontinence.—Laft night, when all
Was funk in deep repofe, a youth I heard
Holding licentious converfe with his comrade,
Of thy fuperior charms; which much he boafted,
As having feen by the broad blaze of day :

Perhaps fome prifoner met thee at the mouth
Of this deep mine?

JULIANA.
Yes, fuch a one I faw,
When firft I trod the defolate abyfs;
Stern was his brow, and dark; as on his feet
They bound the cramping chains, he fmil'd in fcorn;
With more than curious thought he feem'd to eye
And meafure all my form.

FREDERIC.
'Tis he, I doubt not,
Who with uncouth inquiries oft affails me
Touching thy mournful beauty.

JULIANA.
I have mark'd him,
Watchful as if intent on ill; but fure
This gloom will hide me from his diffolute gaze,
And wanton importuning.—What faint gleam
Streams there, in circles of imperfect light?

FREDERIC.

'Tis but the trail of braided sparks, that fly [17]

In quick succession from the whirling flints

And stricken steel; for in this noxious chasm

Such dense and sulphurous fumes exhale, as, touch'd

By lighted torch, would instant fire the air,

And wrap the cavern in continuous blaze.—

But our imperious masters call, and chide

My short delay. May Heaven protect thy weakness!

JULIANA.

Farewell !—This gleam will guide my dubious steps.

See where the livid glare the wretched Count

Discovers, wearied out with loathsome toil ;

To him more loathsome, from remember'd acts

Of generous power, and days of happiest love.

[*Exit* FREDERIC.

JULIANA, CONRAD.

CONRAD.

This way I heard the voice : propitious Fortune

Now brings the fair occasion, which so long

My paffion feeks.   True, fhe's of brighter mould
Than the vile tenants of thefe dreary caves,
And in her eye, as on its natural throne,
Sits noblenefs with melting beauty mix'd:
Like a fequefter'd deer, fhe feems to fhun
The herd of prifoners: yet does her bofom
Heave fighs moft languifhing, and oft I fee her
Beftow officious tendernefs: 'twould make
This drudgery pleafure, could I fhare her charms.
O! why then fhould I doubt it?—Here no bars
Of fcrupulous pride, no decencies forbid,
Nor plighted vows.   I will accoft and prove her.—
Hail! gentle lady, whofe fweet tones have power
To charm away the pangs of fierce defpair,   .
And make night beautiful!—Sure fuch a form,
Fafhion'd with dainty fkill, was never meant
To breathe the vapours of this fpongy vault!

JULIANA.

That foft addrefs fpeaks thee too by harfh fate
Condemn'd to unjuft chaftifement.

CONRAD.

My forrows
Endear to me the wretched. Shall I to-day
Difcharge thy deftin'd tafk of fervile toil?

JULIANA.
'Twere ill to load thee with another's burthen,
Bearing fo much, had not my wafting ftrength
From all laborious works releafe obtain'd.

CONRAD.
Then give fome refpite to thy weary mind,
And woo aufpicious thoughts.

JULIANA.
I fain would do it,
And ever in my prayers remember patience;
For hope of better days attends the good,
And virtue, like the wild-bee, can extract,
E'en from the bitter of adverfity,
Sweet folace.

C

CONRAD.

Thefe grim caves, methinks, fometimes

Forget their horrid nature: I have known them

Blaze with the radiance of ten thoufand ftars,

Shot from invifible firmaments ; while founds,

Surpaffing human fweetnefs, echoed round

The fpangled concave.

JULIANA.

At fuch glorious vifions

I too have marvell'd.

CONRAD.

Why then to delight

Convert we not our fuffering, and thefe crags

To beds of fofteft down ?

JULIANA.

Nay, thou doft wrong

My forrows.

CONRAD.

Rather fay, in that foft form

I read all tendernefs and love.

JULIANA.
Such praiſe
On my cold ear is loſt.   Leave me, I pray thee.

CONRAD.
Not freedom's ſelf ſhould bribe me; were I offer'd
To view the bleſſed ſun, this gloom to change
For populous city, 'midſt delicious fare,
And maſk or amorous feſtival, to thee
I'd cling, nor heed what 'vantages I loſt,
Gaining thy love.

JULIANA.
That couldſt thou never gain.

CONRAD.
Recall that word.

JULIANA.
Think'ſt thou, that entering here,
We loſe each nice and virtuous faculty;
Or vice alone can breathe the unchaſte air?

CONRAD.

Thou doſt increaſe the flame thou mean'ſt to quench,

By ſuch ſweet chiding.

JULIANA.

                    Is each generous ſpark

Blurr'd by theſe ſooty vapours, thus to encounter

My feeble ſpirit ?—There is a majeſty

In humble wretchedneſs, provoking thoſe

Of noble nature to fall down and worſhip.

CONRAD.

    Yes, at thy feet my idolatrous paſſion kneels,

And, like a way-worn pilgrim, joys to claſp

The heavenly ſhrine.

JULIANA.

                    Be gone, raſh youth ! or I

Will raiſe my feeble voice, till every rock

Re-echo to the ſound.

CONRAD.

                    Thy ſtubborn heart

Rejeɛts my proffer'd friendſhip ?

JULIANA.

I defpife
Thy bafe fuggeftions : fooner couldft thou bid
The flow'ret that o'erhangs the ftream, and feeds
On the pure effence, live imprifon'd here,
Than plant true friendfhip in our alien hearts.

CONRAD.

But thou mayft rue my hate, tho' thy proud foul
Swell with imperious fancies of high worth,
Surpaffing frail creation.

JULIANA.

Were I happy,
Thy unjuft menaces would more difturb me.

CONRAD.

There are from whom thy fenfitive referve
Does ne'er recoil. Tell me, haft thou not fat
Motionlefs, while he delv'd the rifted rock ;
Or, when he funk beneath the fultry toil,
Fetch'd the cold beverage, and with gentle hand
Wip'd from his pallid front faint Nature's dew ?

JULIANA.

What fable hath thy angry fancy coin'd?

CONRAD.

Then, as he flept, haft thou not ftol'n towards him,

And hung, in filent gaze, o'er his wan cheek,

That on the chill ftone refted?—Of thefe habits

I will advife our guardian, who, deceiv'd

By thy fair-feeming mien, and gloffing fpeech,

A kind enlargement grants, to us denied.

I'll to him now, and thy o'erweening virtue

He foon fhall recompenfe with meet reward.

[*Exit* CONRAD.

JULIANA.

Oh, Fortune! what new ills haft thou in ftore?

Wilt thou too, like the rude and pitilefs ftorm,

While in the dafhing furge his pinnace finks,

Still beat upon the fhip-wreck'd mariner?—

Ye mazy caverns, fcoop'd with endlefs toil

Beneath the folid rocks, each under each

Projecting, deeper than the wedging root
Of Jove's own oak e'er pierc'd! what do I not
Forego, to dwell within thy dark abode?
Yet of wealth, birth, and the world's flattering gifts,
It recks me not, while in the steady path
Of friendship and of duteous love I tread:
But of that solace should harsh fate bereave me,
Then welcome woe! All other wrongs, to this,
Would seem but as the puling infant's cry
To the loud peal of heaven.—What odours now
Breathe thro' the winding cavern, and o'erpow'r
My drowsy sense? Upon this shelving crag
I will recline, if chance I may obtain
Oblivious respite of intruding care.

Enter the QUEEN, *and* ATTENDANT SPIRITS.

O D E.

I.

Hafte, my Gnomes, your ftrains apply,

And her boding griefs deceive;

Vifions of celeftial dye

In the loom of flumber weave:

Raife before her ravifh'd fight

The pageant of eternal night;

And let her fancy-kindled foul attain

The unknown wonders of our boundlefs reign.

Firft, be with plaftic fceptre feen

The barren Petra, giant queen [18];

Thro' her dun realms let racking cataracts found,

And ocean's billowy ftrength her throne furround:

Each fylph, that floats on ether's wing,

The fading tribes of Flora fling

Beneath her fteps, and, brufh'd by hafty fhow'r,

Strew every quivering leaf, and fhort-liv'd flow'r.

The triumphs of her reign to fwell,

'Midſt buſhy wood and duſky dell,

Bid timorous Fauna chaſe her ſylvan bands,

That howl o'er Zembla's ſnow, or Afric's ſands.

Bring orient Onyx for her zone,

Imperial Granite be her throne ;

While the rich circle of her crown diſplays

The blooming Agat's light, the Opal's purple blaze [19].

II.

Now the central depths unlock,

Where our mineral Druids bend [20],

Muttering o'er each pregnant rock

Magic ſpells, that never end :

Pluck the ethereal tints, that glow

In the cold-ſtreaming lunar bow ;

And o'er the nitrous cavern's icy roof,

In lucid priſms ſuſpend the cryſtal woof.

Command the Phoſphor's kindling ray

To counterfeit the beam of day [21] ;

While Sapphires bright the living fhrine attire,

And Adamant that fcorns the raging fire:

    Then wafted from the frozen deep,

    In Amber's breathing odour fteep

Her flumbering fenfe, and o'er her thrilling frame

Shoot the quick glances of electric flame [22]:

    Unveil the yawning mountain's ftore,

    Each fubject and each fovereign ore [23];

But chief the Solar Lord [24], who dares to wage

High war with elements and devouring age;

    Round him exulting Naiads glide,

    Proud Hermus rolls his turbid tide;

    On folid darknefs his pavilion 's fpread,

While Andes' trembling cliffs re-bellow o'er his head.

III.

Where the fanguine corals fhine,

    In a dripping fea-worn cave,

Let chill Foffilia recline,

    Watching the quick-circling wave [25]:

As her tranflucent fhuttles glance,

The teffellated webs advance ;

Till Nature, refcued by her potent breath,

Exults to perifh, and revives in death.

Her fplendid Talifman can give

Each plant and infect form to live :

Gay birds ftill flutter tho' to marble grown,

The deer's proud antlers branch in wrinkled ftone ;

Impearl'd the fcaly tortoife lies,

While the huge elephant fupplies

His ivory fpoil ; and wreath'd in rocky fold,

The crefted fnake convolves his maze of gold.

Her wizard pencil let her take,

Dipt in the blue and gelid lake,

And as the filmy, bickering colours flow,

Bid fairy fcenes and wild creations glow [26],

Various as clouds on evening gale,

That like deep-burthen'd navies fail,

And labouring o'er the mountain's fhadowy height,

The foreft gloom reflect, the torrent's glittering light.

QUEEN.

Enough, my blest associates! fights like these

With magic charm can harmonize the throbs

Of jealous love, subdue forlorn despair,

And from his treasure the fix'd eye divorce

Of wondering Avarice.—Now watch we well

The arts that subtle malice may devise

To wound unwary innocence; while thus

Wrapt in soft folds of slumber, and inspir'd

By heavenly visions, she suspends her woe.

[*Exeunt the* GNOMES *with their* QUEEN.

JULIANA, COUNT MAURICE.

COUNT MAURICE.

My friend is gone for ever! and in my heart

A void as large has made, as this huge mine

In the earth's centre : yet this dreadful parting,

What is it in the endurance to the thought

Of that o'erwhelming grief, when to the best,

The tenderest of her sex I bade adieu ?

'Twas then the pang, the agony I felt
Of death itfelf, and all fucceeding forrows
Lofe their comparative force.   Yet will I blefs
Juft Heaven, that with a pitying eye regards me,
And in thefe haunts of wretchednefs and guilt
Still leaves me one affociate, whofe firm foul
By hopeful innocence calm'd, looks down on pain,
And fmiles amidft the ghaftly fcene.—Ye rocks,
Witnefs her tender fpirit, her mild zeal,
That blunts affliction's edge !   Sure fhe was fent,
Like a defcending angel, to fupport
My fainting ftrength!—See ! from yon crag fhe bends,
And lifts her drowfy lids, that hang like clouds
Over the brimming ocean, when the fun
Firft peeps from the blue wave.

JULIANA (waking.)

                        Stay, ftay, ye vifions
Of light ineffable !   Aufpicious dreams,
That waft to regions of delight, return
And footh me into reft !

COUNT MAURICE.

My rough intrusion
Disturbs her soft repose.

JULIANA.

What foot approaches?
Where art thou, Guardian Spirit? Lead me on
Thro' worlds of waters, o'er the golden beds
Of virgin ore and sapphire spars, and rocks
Of clustering diamonds. The bright illusion
Flies like the April rack, and I awake
To servitude and darkness.

COUNT MAURICE.

Pardon, Lady,
If my rude tread has broke thy gentle rest.

JU IANA.
Methought my soul o'erleap'd the narrow bounds
Of its dim prison, and wander'd fancy-borne
In subterraneous brightness.

COUNT MAURICE.

Such blest visions
Good angels minister to sleeping virtue.

Stothard del.　　　　　　Neagle sculp.

What foot approaches?
Where art thou, Guardian Spirit? lead me on
Thro' world, of waters,

Published as the Act directs by T. Cadell, Strand, Feb.y 1798.

JULIANA.

Talk not of trivial joys : a blifs more full
From the pure fount of cordial pity flows,
Than dreams or ineffectual fplendors give.

COUNT MAURICE.

And canft thou then, a poor, afflicted creature!
Root from thy heart the fenfe of crowding forrows,
Long days of hope deferr'd, and nights of weeping,
With all the aches and fickening of the foul—
Canft thou forget thy pangs, and on a ftranger
Wafte generous comfort?

JULIANA.

     Some are never ftrangers,
But foon as feen the foul, as 'twere by inftinct,
Springs tow'rds them with refiftlefs force, and owns
Congenial fympathy. Can they who doom us
To bear the load of this degrading thraldom,
Enflave the mind, or the free current check
Of heaven-fprung charity?

COUNT MAURICE.

That pow'r they need not,

Who tear us from the world, and all we love.

JULIANA.

Thou ſtrik'ſt the chord to which my ſad heart

vibrates

In piteous harmony.   Beyond my ſex

I once was bleſt.—How ſhall I tell of him

Who won my love, and winning ſo deſerv'd it ?

For he was all that youthful viſions paint,

Or fancy can pourtray ; each look, each action,

His liberal ſoul expreſs'd, that knew no ebb

Of varying kindneſs.

COUNT MAURICE.

Oh ! what dire remembrance

Has thy ſad ſtory wak'd!—'Twas Heaven's high will,

And I will teach my ſtruggling heart ſubmiſſion.

JULIANA.

In thee I image him, who was my pride,

My life's beſt joy and treaſure ! Why then ſcorn

My willing fervices, and fuch flight tender
Of duteous care as the fond fancy prompts?

Count Maurice.

Sure from the fellowfhip of fuffering virtue
Sweet peace and concord fpring! thy heavenly accents,
Like fhow'rs foft-falling after parching drought,
Refrefh each languid fenfe: when I behold thee
Environ'd by fad forms, pent in the gloom
Of thefe abrupt, unorganized chafms,
'Midft fierce viciffitude of heat and cold
And fublimated vapours, thy meek carriage
Schools me to patience, and exalts my reafon
All vain degenerate weaknefs to fubdue,
And form to thine the temper of my foul.

Juliana.

E'en in thefe unfunn'd caverns we'll difcover
Good unexpected. When thou toil'ft, I'll cheer
The melancholy tafk: each look I'll watch,
And craving figh. Affliction fhall refine

D

Faith's brightening flame, and change our earthly pangs
To golden certainty of heavenly joy.

COUNT MAURICE.
Aid me with thy pure fpirit, and our friendfhip,
By fympathy and virtuous forrows knit,
Shall teach us from the wreck of happinefs
To fave whate'er we can.

JULIANA.
One thought alarms me.
Erewhile, with rude, lafcivious arts, and fhew
Of wanton violence, a rafh youth affail'd me.

COUNT MAURICE.
Villain ! who dar'd to violate the fhrine
By virtue and misfortune facred made !
Had I furpris'd the wretch, his forfeit life
Had quickly for fuch facrilege aton'd.

JULIANA.
Nay, check thy hafty rage : think what a crew,
Outcafts and ruthlefs bandits, fojourn here ;

And rather by wife caution fhun, than fteel
Their defperate cruelty. Ere he departed,
He mutter'd fome dark threats, that he'd report
Our loves (for fo he term'd them—much, I ween,
Unus'd to virtuous friendfhip) to the guard
Of this our prifon. 'Twere well now to retire,
Left, ftung by jealous rage, Conrad return,
And in this folitary nook o'ertake us.

[*Exeunt.*

CONRAD.

Thus far has fortune crown'd me with fuccefs:
In the fufpicious ear of him who rules
This dungeon, fuch quick poifon have I pour'd,
That to the loweft depths of this vaft mine
He dooms Count Maurice, and now bids me bear him
His rigorous command. The lazy vapours
Of thofe dank caves will rid me of my rival :
Then may I furely practife on the ear

Of the fair prifoner.—To the Count I'll fpeed,

And when I've greeted him with my ftern warrant,

I'll feek his beauteous friend, who of her love

Bereft, no more may chance to coy it with me.

[*Exit.*

The *found of the Miners is heard in various parts, and*
feveral of them crofs the ftage, fome with tools, others
with maffes of ftone and ore: after which, the
GNOMES *and their* QUEEN *enter.*

O D E.

I.

Mortals! tho' you toil for ever,

Never fhall your labours, never

Our effential realms unfold [27];

Where, in impenetrable night,

We make conflicting elements unite,

And build eternal fhrines of Amaranthine gold.

II.

Think not, when our bolts you hear,

We in rage vindictive joy :

Or when furging flames appear,

That we triumph to deftroy [28]:

Thro' the reluctant rocks we pour

The living current of each lingering ore,

And with the blaze

Of folar rays

Light in the dark gem all his liquid fire;

That you to virtue may afpire,

To patient induftry your pow'rs conform [29],

And withering floth fubdue, and paffion's wayward

ftorm.

III.

Our wealth, our boons profufe,

To your admiring hands we give;

The flaming fpoil, ye heirs of joy ! receive,

And fanctify by virtuous ufe.

Nor let ingenuous Penury defpair :

To her what bounteous gifts we deal by ſtealth!

When each fierce pang we ſooth, and bid her ſhare

Of eaſe the treaſure, and the gems of health [30].

Toil then, ye wondering mortals! and confeſs,

That heaven above was made, and earth below, to bleſs.

Enter a party of GNOMES, *returning from their works,*
and ſinging.

Now our golden taſks are done,

Hurry, ſpirits! hurry on,

With feſtive revelry to join

Our Sovereign in this ſparkling mine.

Quick as light from heavenly ſphere

We have run our wide career;

With fleet ſtep pac'd our midnight way [31],

And ruſh'd to meet the morning ray;

Beneath the Caſpian we have ſtood,

And croſs'd the Magellanic flood;

In glittering labyrinths have led
The Naiads o'er their rocky bed,
And taught the bright ores, as they rove,
To challenge each his mineral love [32].
Saw ye, wherefoe'er we ftept,
How the confcious Dryads wept,
And perifh'd as we fleeted by ?—
Shall they dare with us to vie [35] ?
Tho' the oak's gigantic form
Tow'r, and grapple with the ftorm,
Soon it totters in decay,
To the mining worm a prey.
But our adamantine toil
All the rage of Time can foil ;
And Death, with univerfal pow'rs,
Submiffive minifters to ours.

QUEEN.

Welcome, bright minifters ! whofe gorgeous toils
And alchymy demand eternal praife;
Nor lefs entitle you to fuch high reft

And glorious recreation, as becomes

Tranfcendent fpirits.—But firft with us partake

The joy divine that waits us, when from depths

Of whelming mifery we a generous youth

To unexpected liberty fhall raife,

And boundlefs blifs : for my returning Gnomes

I now behold, who by our kind beheft,

With fpeed immortal to his fovereign borne,

In the rich fplendor of her blazing ring,

Beryl and flaming chryfolite, have hid

Their glittering effence, and with heavenly fkill

Have fhot the beams of mercy o'er her foul.

[*Exeunt the* GNOMES *with their* QUEEN.

COUNT MAURICE, JULIANA.

JULIANA.
This moment, didft thou fay ?

COUNT MAURICE.
This very moment :
I read the fell decree, and muft obey.

JULIANA.

Mifcreant! who in my chafte ear dar'd to breathe

His bafe, licentious vows; and now on thee

Wreaks barbarous vengeance!

COUNT MAURICE.

We are thrown among

Traitors and murderers. But the inflicted ill

Bears its own cure: the damp infectious air

Will quickly fet me free.

JULIANA.

That dreadful thought

Weighs down my foul with grief! 'Twas I that did it.

Pardon my weak, rafh tendernefs!—I meant

To have made the lonefome hours of fore reftraint

Glide on with brifker ftep.

COUNT MAURICE.

And for thy friendfhip,

If my big heart permit, I fain would thank thee.

JULIANA.

Is this an hour for parley? No, I'll fly,

Unmaſk the covert wretch who has betray'd us,

And to our regent's eye diſplay the clear

And palpable diſſembling of his falſehood:

He is not of ſo ſtern a caſt, ſo ſteel'd

By his obdurate office, but he'll liſten

To pity and to truth.

COUNT MAURICE.
Reſtrain thy anguiſh,

Nor waſte kind pains on one whom Heaven chaſtiſes—

One from mankind ſelected to endure

A double weight of woe.   Now farewell hope!

Farewell thou upper world, and all thou holdeſt!

Dear ſource of vain regret, my loves, my friendſhips,

That tie this ſoul to earth!—But I'll be patient.

Ye eyes, forget to weep!   Whate'er in future

Dread tortures threaten, be the paſt my refuge:

There thy exalted thoughts, thy acts I'll trace

Of charity and love divine.—O give me

Some portion of thy meek, forbearing ſpirit,

And let me in my memory's deepeſt folds,

Mix'd with each gentle deed, record thy virtues!
If ever we fhould meet again—

JULIANA.

Ah! where,
Where fhould we ever meet?—My tender frame
Pines daily to decay ; and palfied age
E'en on the threfhold of green youth o'ertakes me [34].

COUNT MAURICE.
One parting pray'r accept : Let me ftill live
In thy remembrance, tho' I nought deferve it ;
For oft with moody filence I've requited
Thy generous folace : but infatiate grief
And lofs of friends almoft to madnefs urg'd me.
Pardon, fweet Lady! and may each pitying faint
Heal thy fad fpirit, and reward thy goodnefs !

JULIANA.
Oh ! my poor trembling heart can ne'er fuftain
This exquifite affliction !—But I'll try
What tears, what bribes may do.

[*Exit* JULIANA.

COUNT MAURICE.

Go, thou kind angel!

Go, tho' thy pains be fruitlefs. Hark! I'm fummon'd.

Welcome, ye deepeft horrors! I am arm'd

With ftern defpair, and can defy you all.

Enter LEOPOLD.

COUNT MAURICE, LEOPOLD.

COUNT MAURICE.

Who's here?—What, Leopold! art thou return'd

To double all my torments?

LEOPOLD.

I am come

To heal thefe agonies, and bear thee back

To liberty and light.

COUNT MAURICE.

Is it then true,

Or all a mocking dream? Tell me!—O fpeak!—

LEOPOLD.

Thro' the dark mazes of perplexing malice
Thy fovereign has pierc'd. Scarce had I trod,
With many a weary ftep, the long afcent,
And on my aching eyes the day-beam beat,
When the quick meffenger I met, who bore
The gracious tidings; and a livelier joy
O'erwhelm'd my foul, than when they firft pronounc'd
My own deliverance.

COUNT MAURICE.
My deareft friend!

Long be our days of happinefs and freedom!
But tell me, Leopold—my wife—how fares fhe?
In the lone filence of fome hallow'd cloyfter,
Say, has fhe hid her unexampled woes,
Far from the faithlefs court and world's turmoil?
How brook'd fhe her fad folitude?

LEOPOLD.
Oh Maurice!—

Count Maurice.

Why that blank paufe?—that look?—Yes, in thine

   eye

The harrowing tale I read: her fuffering 's clos'd.

Leopold.

Truft in all-righteous Heaven.

Count Maurice.

       Then lives fhe yet?

Leopold.

Cherifh not fanguine hope, nor yet deplore her

As one thou'rt doom'd ne'er to behold again.

From the dread hour the minifters of force

Divorc'd thee from her, fhe refus'd all comfort,

And feem'd to feed upon her grief. One morning

In compos'd mood fhe rofe, and made pretence

To tafte the fweet air of the neighbouring meads:

But ne'er did fhe return; nor could thy friends

With anxious, endlefs fearch detect her flight.

COUNT MAURICE.

Greet me no more with pardon! leave me here

To delve the rugged rocks, and let me labour

Till toil and extreme mifery releafe me

From this deep wretchednefs.

LEOPOLD.

Think, think of freedom,

Nor mock juft Heaven with fuch unmeet defpair.

COUNT MAURICE.

My firm refufal of her generous purpofe

To fhare the burthen of this torturing yoke,

Diftracted her weak fpirit, and 'gainft herfelf

Arm'd her precipitate grief.—Yet witnefs, Heaven,

How much I lov'd her! In my bittereft moments,

Her melancholy and unprotected ftate

O'erwhelm'd me with frefh anguifh.—To the world

I now return, bereft of every hope,

As one expos'd in a huge wildernefs,

Who eyes in mute defpair the hideous void.

LEOPOLD.

Away with this intemperance of grief!

Count Maurice.

Or deeming me, perhaps, for ever loft—
Thought worfe than death!—fhe to another has given
That heart which only I could fill, and pledg'd
Her plighted faith.

Juliana (*returning, and throwing afide her veil.*)
Never, oh never fpeak it!
For thee alone fhe lives! Behold thy true,
Thy faithful Juliana!

Count Maurice.
Gracious fpirits!
Ye heavenly powers proteft me!

Juliana.
Here behold her,
Whom love a voluntary flave detains.

Count Maurice.
Do I then fee thee, or do earthly goblins
Vex me with vain illufions?

Stothard del.   Hall sculp.

Never, oh never speak it!
For thee alone she lives! Behold thy true,
Thy faithful Juliana!

Published as the Act directs by T. Cadell, Strand, Feb.ʸ 11788.

JULIANA.

With feign'd accents
No more I cheat thine ear : turn then towards me,
And bleſs me with one look of wonted fondneſs.

COUNT MAURICE.

Yes, thou art ſhe ! and thus my heart unſays
That unkind thought, and clafps thee never more
To part again. Oh! what muſt thou have borne,
Pent in thefe murky cells, 'midſt loathfome vice !
Tell me, why didſt thou hide thyſelf ſo long ?
Why from my weeping eyes conceal thy beauty
Beneath thefe dripping weeds and fervile garb ?

JULIANA.

How often have I long'd into thy arms
To ſpring, and tell thee all ! but well I knew
Thy generous nature never would confent
That I ſhould dwell within this baleful dungeon :
Yet other ſpots were as a dreary defart ;
And thefe damp, low-brow'd rocks, cheer'd by thy
        preſence,
Seem'd fumptuous palaces.

E

LEOPOLD.
        Tranfcendent love!

JULIANA.
One happy look of thine o'erpays an age
Of doleful penance.

        COUNT MAURICE.
        Greatly haft thou fuffer'd!
But fhades of paft misfortune fhall fet off
Our brighter days. Come, let us now afcend—
For we have much to fay, and my glad heart
Swells with fuch raptures as it ne'er can utter. [*Ex.*

Enter the QUEEN, *and* ATTENDANT SPIRITS.

Come, my triumphant Gnomes, who like the fun
Thro' the vaft concave your fleet courfe have run;
Whofe cars, felf-rolling, fcorn the bounding fteed,
While nymphs and fiery falamanders lead;
No more your glittering myriads now employ,
But give my fubterraneous realm to joy.
What tho' for us no circling feafons glide,
No fprings luxuriant lavifh all their pride;

In earth's brute caverns we can wake delight,
And gild with rapture the dark brow of night.
Thro' scenes as fair as those above we'll go,
And meet a brighter universe below.
See where our vallies wind, our Alps arise,
What meteors thwart, what suns emblaze the skies!
Here foaming cataracts the wild champaign shake,
There in diffusive radiance sleeps the lake;
Huge caves expand [35], thro' whose wide-yawning arch
Embattled hosts of mightiest kings can march;
The shadowy void deep-brooding darkness fills,
And smooths her plumage in the dripping rills;
In frowning state self-center'd columns glare,
Abortive echoes flutter in the air;
Their dusky foliage rocks fantastic wreath,
And quake, like forests, to the blasts beneath:
These scenes each fierce, presumptuous thought controul,
And rouse to ecstasy the slumbering soul.
Let Elfin Faies expect the dewy hours,
And their quaint morrice weave in moonlight bow'rs;

Let ſportive Nymphs purſue each dancing ſpring,

And ſhouting Dryads make the foreſt ring ;

In fields of ether Sylphs exulting trip,

Or in the galaxy their pinions dip :

Our taſks perform'd, ſublimer joys abound ;

In mute and reverend awe we watch around,

Woo contemplation from the thrones of bliſs,

And ſhew rapt wiſdom all the vaſt abyſs.

Nor thrills not dreadful harmony our ear,

When the great deep's careering flood we hear ;

Or ſtruggling vapours vollied thunder urge,

And Nature trembles on her utmoſt verge [36].

Such joys ſevere, with heavenly muſing fraught,

Wake the ſtill energies of virtuous thought,

Teach us the wealth of reaſon to adore

Beyond each dazzling gem, or barren ore ;

And, as we miniſter at Nature's ſhrine,

To be in goodneſs, as in pow'r, divine.

NOTES

ON

THE MINE.

Note 1, Page 3.

THE spirited and loyal support which the late Empress Maria Theresa received from her Hungarian subjects, when she was driven from her capital by her enemies, is well known. Their singular exclamation on that occasion is still remembered: " Moriamur pro rege nostro Maria Theresa!"

Note 2, Page 6.

That inimitable poem, The Rape of the Lock, has made the system of the Rosicrusians, it is

prefumed, familiar to every one. Thofe fpecu-
lative alchymifts revived the old Platonic philofophy ; and not only appropriated peculiar fpirits to the air and water, but fuppofed even
fire and the deepeft receffes of the earth, to have
their fpiritual inhabitants. Πολλα δαιμονων γενη,
και ϖαντοδαπα τας ιδεας και τα σωματα, ως ειναι
ϖληρη μεν τον αερα, τον τε 'υπερθεν ήμων και τον
ϖερι ήμας, ϖληρη δε γχιαν και θαλατlαν, και τhs
μυχαιτατως και βυθιhs τοπhs. (Michael Pfellus,
p. 41.)—The fpirits, who were fuppofed by the
Roficrufians to inhabit the earth, received from
them the name of Gnomes. So congenial is it
to the human mind to affociate the idea of fuper-
natural agents with darknefs and the wonders of
the fubterraneous world, that fuch fuperftitious
notions are generally found to prevail among the
people who inhabit the mine countries. Thofe
of Idria, in particular, we learn from Keyfler,
are not exempt from this weaknefs. " As the

inhabitants of all mine towns have their ftories
of goblins, fo are the people here ftrongly poffeffed with a notion of fuch apparitions that
haunt the mines. It is faid that the miners of
Idria have formerly been fo fuperftitious, as to
fet fome provifions for the mine fpirit every
day, in order to render him propitious and fa-
vourable to them. It is added, that every year
they hung up a red fuit of clothes in one of the
paffages of the mine. This little old man with
a great head (for that is the fhape he generally
affumes) is faid not to fhew himfelf fo frequently
fince annual proceffions have been performed
with the Hoft, and the Monks have confecrated
thofe places, where he ufed to be moft mif-
chievous, with holy water and other ceremonies.
However, they ftill believe that he fometimes
knocks when they are at work in the mines;
upon which they immediately leave off, having,
as they pretend, often experienced, that, if they

do not immediately lay by their tools out of respect to the goblin, but continue to work in opposition to him, some misfortune or other never fails to happen to them for their presumption." Keysler's Travels, vol. iii. p. 377.—To this popular superstition of the Miners, our great Poet alludes in his Comus:

" No Goblin or swart Fairy of the Mine
" Hath hurtful power o'er true virginity."

Note 3, Page 7.

Gold, by the chymists, is styled Sol et Rex Metallorum, The Sun and Sovereign of Metals. —See the second of Dr. Wall's Dissertations on Chymistry and Medicine, in which he explains how the symbols of Astronomy were transferred to Alchymy, and why each sign was appropriated to its respective metal.

Note 4, Page 8.

Gold is never found in the state of a true ore, unless when blended with a *large proportion* of other metals. The chief mines of it, it is well known, are in South America.

Note 5, Page 8.

Silver, by the chymists, is styled Diana Metallorum. Platina, a new metal lately discovered in the gold mines of the Spanish West Indies, resembles it much in colour, though in other respects it comes nearer to gold. The Count de Buffon indeed is of opinion, that Platina is not a new metal, but only a natural mixture of gold and iron. See an account of his experiments, Supplement à l' Histoire Naturelle, tom. i. p. 301. —Mr. Kirwan, with more propriety, has arranged it among the metals next to gold.

Note 6, Page 8.

Lead and Copper; the one called Saturn, the other Venus, by the chymifts. The noxious effects of the former have been inveftigated with fagacity and precifion by Sir George Baker, Medic. Tranf. vol. i. and ii. The ores of the latter are often of the moft brilliant colours, being variegated like the rainbow or peacock's tail.

Note 7, Page 8.

Iron, by the chymifts, is denominated Mars; and is well known, when infufed in water, to conftitute the chalybeate fprings, applied to fo many purpofes of health. The phænomenon of its attraction by the magnet is very familiar, and has been frequently alluded to and defcribed by the poets. The lines of Claudian on that fubject are not worthy of him; but the Author of the Poem, Περι Λιθων, which (without the leaft ground indeed of reafon or probability) has been imputed to Orpheus, has defcribed the magnet in a beautiful manner. However his tafte might be degraded by the age in which he lived, his imagination was rich and elegant. The conjecture of Mr. Tyrwhit in the following paffage, with a fimplicity that befpeaks its truth, at once corrects the fenfe, and rectifies the metre:

Τολμα δ' αθαναίνς και εηεϊ μειλισσεσθαι

Μαγησα· την δ' εξοχ' εφιλαίο θυριος Αρης

'Ουνεκεν οππόΙε κεν πελασοι πολιοιο σιδηρu,

Ηϋτε παρθενικη γλαγοφρον χερσιν ελνσα

Ηίθεον στερνω προσπίνσσεται ίμερόεντι,

Ωs ήγ' άρπαζεσα ποίι σφέιερον δεμαs αιει,

Και παλιν εκ εθελει μεθεμεν πολεμιςα σιδηρον.

Περι Λιθων, ver. 301.—κτλ.

Immortal minds the Magnet can delight,
And Mars exulting owns his potent might;

For when the near approach you bid him feel,

His powers attractive fix the quivering steel :

And as a maid, who first reveals her charms,

Clasps her dear lover in her trembling arms,

To his fond breast he draws, to part no more,

And holds with ardent grasp the martial ore.

Note 8, Page 8.

The globules of Mercury divide upon touch into numerous smaller ones; the minutest of which, that can be distinguished by the naked eye, appear perfect specula, reflecting very vividly the images of neighbouring objects.

Note 9, Page 9,

The different elastic fluids existing in metals, and other substances, have lately attracted the attention of philosophers; whose discoveries, particularly those of Dr. Priestley, are infinitely curious and important. A general account of them is to be found in Sir John Pringle's elegant Difcourfe on that fubject. Dr. White has, by numerous experiments, demonftrated how much the effluvia of bogs or marfhes diminifh the air. He gives a dreadful inftance indeed of this, in the diabolical revenge of the Arabs; who, when they think themfelves injured by the Turks at Baffora, break down the banks of the river, and lay all its environs under water. As the water evaporates, the mud and other impurities fo vitiate the air, as to caufe a moft mortal fever in that populous city. This was the cafe when Mr. Ives was there: — of this fever fourteen thoufand fouls perifhed; and of the Europeans fettled there, only three efcaped with life. —A moft horrid mode of revenge! and a dreadful example of the deadly effects of marfhes and ftagnant waters in hot climates. — Philof. Tranf. vol. lxviii. p. 194.

Note 10, Page 9.

There is a lake in the diftrict of Bolellaw, in Bohemia, that contains many gulfs of a depth which it is impoflible to fathom ; and from whence it frequently happens that fuch impetuous hurricanes afcend, as blow over the whole country, and in the winter force away in their paffage pieces of ice of above a hundred weight.—Act. Lipf. Anno 1682, p. 246.—Buffon, Hift. Nat. tom. i. p. 427.

Note 11, Page 9.

Pliny relates that the lake Trafymenus took fire, and burnt for fome time. — Hift. Nat. lib. ii. c. 107.

Note 12, Page 9.

One of the moft extraordinary volcanic mountains is Cotopaxi, in the province of Quito : it is three miles perpendicular above the level of the fea; and the found of one of its eruptions was heard at 150 miles diftance. In 1742, M. M. Bouger and Condamine were witneffes of a dreadful inundation, occafioned by the fnow on the top of the mountain being melted by the heat of the volcano.—See Voyage par M. M. Bouger & Condamine, pour determiner la Figure de la Terre, p. 68; and Ulloa, vol. i. p. 442.

Note 13, Page 9.

Numberlefs are the inftances of iflands being formed by fubterraneous fires.—Plin. Hift. Nat. lib. ii. c. 36, 37.—Buffon, Hift. Nat. tom. i. p. 536.—Philof. Tranf. vol. v. p. 197.

Note 14, Page 9.

Such accidents in the Andes are not uncommon.—Buffon, Hift. Nat. tom. i. p. 550.—This fpeftacle indeed has been recently exhibited in all its terrors.—See a Letter from Sir William

Hamilton to the Royal Society, giving an account
of the late earthquake in Calabria and Sicily.

NOTE 15, Page 10.

The ftreams in the mines are tinged with different fubftances : fome are whitifh and milky, being
impregnated with Lac Lunæ, or the Milk of
Silver.—See Dr. Browne's Travels to the Mine
Towns in Hungary, p. 57.

NOTE 16, Page 11.

The earth in fome parts of Arabia, upon being
dug, emits odoriferous fteams.—Diodor. Sicul. lib.
ii. p. 132. edit. Rhodomani. Some of the moft
noxious vapours in the mines are alfo attended with
a delightful fmell, refembling the pea-bloffom. It
generally comes in the fummer, and obliges the
miners to quit their work, to whom it would other-
wife foon prove fatal.—Philof. Tranf. Lowthorpe's
Abrid. vol. ii. p. 375.

NOTE 17, Page 19.

The vapours in fome of the mines prevent the introduction of lighted candles or lamps ; in which cafe they have recourfe to the following contrivance :—There is a wheel, the circumference of which is befet with flints ; which ftriking againft fteels placed for that purpofe at the extremity, a ftream of fire is produced, which affords a fufficient light for the operation of the miners.— Goldfmith's Hiftory of Animated Nature, vol. i. p. 82.

NOTE 18, Page 28.

The *Petræ*, or barren ftony fubftances, according to Linnæus, form the firft divifion of the foffil kingdom. They are produced by the earth of vegetables, the earth of animals, the vifcid fediment of the fea, and the precipitation of rain water.—Linnæi Syftema Naturæ, vol iii. p. 34. ———In this poetical delineation of the foffil kingdom, though the Author has followed the fyftem of Linnæus, he does not mean to infinuate any unjuft preference of that fyftem to the more accurate arrangement which is to be met with in the writings of Wallerius, Cronftedt, and Bergman; and particularly in the fcientific treatife of our own countryman, Mr. Kirwan, on this fubject.— See Elements of Mineralogy, by Richard Kirwan, Efquire.

NOTE 19, Page 29.

These ftones are the moft valuable that belong to the order of Petræ. The Onyx is a native of the Eaft. The Opal is defcribed by Linnæus, reflectione purpurafcens, refractione ruber, venis violaceis. The beauty of it did not efcape the author of the poem Περι Λιθων.

Φημι δε τοι τερπειν και Οπαλλιον ϋρανιωνας

Αγλαον ἱμερϋ τερενα χροα ϖαιδος εχοντα.

Ver. 279.

Ye Gods! the Opal ye furvey with joy,

Whofe fplendor blufhes like a blooming boy.

In order to obtain a ftone of this fort, which was in the poffeffion of Nonius, a Roman Senator, and valued at 20,000 fefterces, Pliny fays that Anthony profcribed him.

Note 20, Page 29.

The *Mineræ*, or prolific ftony fubftances, conftitute the fecond divifion of the foffil kingdom, and are all produced by cryftallization. Of this clafs are the precious gems and metals.—Linnæi Syft. Nat. vol. iii. p. 81.

Note 21, Page 29.

The Muria Phofphorea of Linnæus, which is found near Bologna and in China.

Note 22, Page 30.

The Amber and Succinum Electricum are included in the clafs of Mineræ. The latter is formed in the Baltic, and is dug out of the ground in Pruffia and Siberia.—Linnæus obferves that the electric matter was firft difcovered by it: indeed the fcience in general has received its name from this fubftance.—See Prieftley's Hiftory of Electricity.

NOTE 23, Page 30.

The metals are diftinguifhed into perfect or imperfect, according to their capacity of refifting fire.

NOTE 24, Page 30.

It has been remarked before, that Gold is ftyled the Sun or Sovereign of Metals. The river Hermus was indebted for its gold to the Pactolus, which received the golden particles from the mines of mount Tmolus. Celebrated as they formerly were for this quality, by the accounts of Smith, Wheler, and Spon, they are now totally deprived of it.—See Recherches fur le Pactole, Hiftoire de l'Academie des Infcr. tom.

xxi. p. 19.————So great has been the eagernefs of man to poffefs this metal, that, if we can believe an old Greek fcholiaft, he has even made minute and contemptible infects fubfervient to his avarice. Εςι δε κ͗ εν τῇ 'Ινδια τόπος χρυσε ψήγμαλα ἔχων, ὃν ἀνορύτλεσι Θηρία τινα μυρμηκες καλεμενα, τοιεροῖς χρώμενα, ἀφ' ὧν οἱ Ινδοι μηχαναῖς τισι λαμβανεσι τον χρυσον.—Sophocles Antigone Scholiaft, to ver. 1050.

NOTE 25, Page 30.

The *Foffilia* is the laft divifion of the foffil kingdom, and includes all the petrifactions.— Linnæi Syft. Nat. vol. iii. p. 153.————The procefs of petrifaction is defcribed by the Author of the Poem Περι Λιθων, in a manner peculiarly happy :

Αυλη δ'εν βενθεσσιν 'υπο φλοισ͂οιο θαλασσης

Νηχελαι, οφρα κυμαλ' αποπλυσοι αιγιαλονδε

. . . .

Δηρον δ' ε μιλεπελα ταγῳ τεριπαχυνθεισι

Πείρυται, και χερσιν εν οκριοεντα τεησιν

Αμφαφαεις λιθον, ὁ πριν εχων υγρον δεμας ηεν·

Σχημα μεν ον βολαης ετι ὁι μενει, ὁιον εην περ,

Οιτε κλαδοι, ὁσα τε σφιν ακρουρυα προσπεφυασι,

Ἡτε ὁι εβλαςησε και ετραφη εις ἁλι ῥιζα·

Φλοιος δ᾽ ὁσπερ εην, φλοιος κεν λαινος εςι.

Ver. 516.

Torn from the caves profound where oceans roar,

And toſt by billows on the jutting ſhore,

His wounded roots the coral to repair,

Dries on the beach, and petrifies in air.

The hardening plant his branching ſhape retains,

On his ſtiff rind diſplays meand'ring veins;

Seems on the rocky margin to have grown,

And ſhines with leaves of vegetable ſtone.

Note 26, Page 31.

The various vegetables, animals, &c. that are
found in a petrified ſtate, may be ſeen in Lin-

næus. Some petrifactions, such as the Grapto-
lithus, are remarkable for picturefque beauty, re-
prefenting landfcapes with woods and water, or
defolate regions with buildings in ruin.—Linnæi
Syft. Nat. vol. iii. p. 173.

Note 27, Page 40.

A gnat, fays an ingenious writer, effaying the
feeble effects of its flender probofcis againft the
hide of an elephant, and attempting thereby to
inveftigate the internal formation of the body of
that huge animal, is no unapt reprefentation of
man attempting to explore the internal ftructure
of the earth, by digging fmall holes on its fur-
face.—Watfon's Chemical Effays, vol. i. p. 184.
——Monf. de Maupertuis, with the vivacity of
his country, but with a fpirit unbecoming a true
philofopher, propofed to fink a fhaft through the
centre of the earth to the antipodes. — In the
mean while, our difcoveries of its interior parts

are very limited. The deepeſt mine at Cotte-
berg, in Hungary, reaches only three thouſand
feet, and bears no proportion to the depth of
the globe. This undiſcovered ſpace is filled according to the conjectures of ſpeculative men.—
Compare the hypotheſes of Boyle, Whiſton, Bur-
net, Kircher, and Buffon.

Note 28, Page 41.

Such phænomena, though alarming to the ig-
norant, have ſometimes led to very fortunate
diſcoveries. A Wallachian, ſays Baron Born,
whoſe name was Armenian John, came to my
father, then poſſeſſed of a rich ſilver mine at
Cſertes, telling him, that as he conſtantly ob-
ſerved a flame iſſuing from, and playing upon a
fiſſure in the Nagyag foreſt, he was of opinion
that rich ores muſt be hid under ground. My
father was fortunately adventurous enough to
liſten to this poor man's tale; and accordingly

he drove a gallery in the ground which the Wallachian had pointed out. The work went on
fome years without any fuccefs, and my father
refolved to give it up : however he made a laft
drift towards the fiffure, and there he hit the
rich black and lamellated gold ores, which firft
were looked upon as iron glimmer, but appeared
what really they are, as foon as affayed by fire. This
happy accident caufed my father to purfue the work
to the utmoft of his power : accordingly he diftri-
buted fome fhares among his friends, and had the
works carried on with regularity.—Travels through
the Bannat of Temefwar, by Baron Born, Letter xi.
p. 97.

Note 29, Page 41.

Notwithftanding the exaggerated accounts of the
Peruvians, which have been expofed by an able and
philofophic writer, fo neceffary are the metals to the
happinefs of man, that he cannot exift, except in a
ftate of barbarifm, without them.—See Recherches

Philofophiques fur les Americains, tom. ii. p. 204.

NOTE 30, Page 41.

The author of the poem Περι Λιθων afcribes fome properties to minerals, which, fortunately for mankind, they do not poffefs (fee ver. 312). But though they are void of thefe imaginary qualities, they fupply us with the moft active and ufeful medicines ; and both the wifdom and goodnefs of Providence are equally confpicuous in the final caufes of the foffil kingdom.

NOTE 31, Page 41.

The numerous veins in the mines are divided, according to their directions, into *midnight* or *morning veins ;* the former running from South to North, the latter from Eaft to Weft.—See Mr. J. J. Ferber's Mineralogical Hiftory of Bohemia, p. 257.

NOTE 32, Page 42.

Water faturated with mineral particles enters
the hollows and fiffures of rocks; and when it
evaporates, the minerals unite according to their
refpective affinities.

NOTE 33, Page 42.

——————————— μεγα μεν σθενος επλετο ριζης
Αλλα λιθϑ πολυ μειζον· επει μενος αφθιλον αιει
Γεινομενῳ μητηρ και αγηραον εγγυαλιξεν.

Περι Λιθων, ver. 404.

What tho' in air the tree umbrageous fhoots,
And grafps the folid earth with ftedfaft roots?
Superior gems his tottering bulk furvey,
And blaze unhurt, while ages roll away.

Minerals are known to be peculiarly deftruc-
tive to all vegetable productions.—Mr. Pennant,
fpeaking of the vaft copper mine in the Ifle of

Anglesey, obferves, " The whole afpect of this tract has by the mineral operations assumed a most savage appearance. Suffocating fumes of the burning heaps of copper arife in all parts, and extend their baneful influence for miles around. In the adjacent parts vegetation is nearly deftroyed; even the mosses and the lichens of the rocks have perished; and nothing feems capable of refifting the fumes, but the purple Melic grafs (Aira Cœrulea, Hudson's Flor. Angl.) which flourishes in abundance."—Tour into Wales, vol. ii.

Note 34, Page 47.

Mr. Bowles and Don Ant. Ulloa have endeavoured to extenuate the evil effects of the mines upon thofe who work in them : but the unwholefomenefs of them in general, and of the quickfilver mines in particular, is established by the cleareft proof. It appears by a memorial prefented to

Philip III. in the year 1609, that in every
diftrict of Peru, where the Indians are compelled to labour in the mines, their numbers were
reduced to the half, and in fome places to the third,
of what it was in 1581.—Robertfon's Hift. of
America, vol. iii. note 53.——Dr. Pope, who
vifited the mines at Idria in 1664, affures us that
all the labourers, fooner or later, become paralytic,
and die hectic. He faw a man who had not been
in the mines for above half a year before, and who
was fo full of mercury, that upon putting a piece
of brafs in his mouth, or rubbing it in his fingers,
it immediately became white, as if he had rubbed
mercury upon it.—Philof. Tranf. Lowthorpe's
Abrid. vol. ii. p. 580.

NOTE 35, Page 55.

See the defcriptions of Oakey Hole, Pen-park
Hole, the Grotto of Antiparos, and other fubterraneous cavities. One of the moft extraordinary is
that mentioned by Œlian, in the country of the

Arrian Indians, who made a practice of plunging a great number of different animals in the horrible chasm, to satisfy their barbarous superstition.— Œliani Var. Hist. lib. xvi. cap. 16.

NOTE 36, Page 55.

On the first of November, 1755, when the great earthquake happened at Lisbon, a violent noise was heard in the mines in Derbyshire; and from the extent of that earthquake, it is conjectured that this subterraneous thunder must have been heard above three thousand miles.—See Whitehurst on the Formation of the Earth, and Mr. Michell's Treatise on Earthquakes.

THE

VISION OF STONEHENGE,

AN ODE:

Occafioned by a tradition that Charles II. paffed
the night there in his flight from the battle of
Worcefter.—Dryden alludes, in his Epiftle to
Dr. Charleton, to this circumftance, in the following lines :

Thefe ruins fhelter'd once his facred head,
When he from Worcefter's fatal battle fled;
Watch'd by the Genius of this royal place,
And mighty vifions of the Danifh race.

DRYDEN's POEMS, vol. ii. p. 154.

THE

VISION OF STONEHENGE;

AN ODE.

Ταυτ' εμοιγε δειμα τ' εστ' ιδειν
Τμιν δ' ακηειν.　　　Æsch.

I.

SEE, Worcester! fee thy blood-ftain'd walls;

  England, mourn thy warriors flain!

In vain their vanquifh'd fovereign calls,

  No more they rife again.——

Where'er the mingled banners fly,

  Forms of grifly havoc glare,

Shrieks of deathful agony

  Shake the earth and rend the air:

With hafty flight, and Heav'n his guide,

He fcours the folitary champaign wide,

Still feems of battle the loud din to hear,

While fteeds and clattering arms re-echo in his ear.

II.

The heavens, as confcious of fuch feuds,

    Redden with indignant light ;

While terror in the tempeft broods,

    And deepens low'ring night :

To the huge plain at length he comes,

    Spreading wide to Sarum's fpire ;

O'er the pile gigantic roams,

    Gleaming with meteorous fire :

Then pillows on the rocky bed

In fore difmay his faint afflicted head ;

Portentous vifions fcare his clofing eyes,

And mighty warriors march and Britifh kings arife.

III.

With crown that hangs like vapor pale
   Round a dim autumnal ftar,
Stern Harold [1] bids the monarch hail,
   And fhews his Norman fcar.——
A victim of the fylvan fight [2],
   Lifts his purple-ftreaming creft,
And with more than mortal might
   Tears the arrow from his breaft.
With holy palms from Syria won,
Behold, fad Eleanor, thy bleeding fon [3];
With proud Carnarvon's heir [4], whofe forrows fharp
From echoing Severn found and Cambria's mid-
    night harp.

IV.

Behind a form, whofe haggard eyes
   From their fiery fockets burft,
Up ftarts, and fpeaks with endlefs fighs
   Unconquerable thirft [5]:

With trembling ftep, but fainted mien,

    Martyr'd Lancafter appears [6];

By his fide a Prince is feen [7]

    Smiling through his youthful tears:

In wildeft ftorm of paffion toft,

And circled with a dark and fhadowy hoft,

Stalks murderous Richard [8], and new horror flings

O'er the enfanguined crowd of agonizing kings.

V.

In the long rear of royal dead

    Gleams his fire's grief-harrow'd face;

O'er his fix'd lineaments is fhed

    A pale and penfive grace:

Before him, tho' mad factions bray,

    With fond heart and ftedfaft eye,

Dauntlefs Strafford leads the way

    Of thundering deftiny:

To a meek faint [9], who fmiles above,

One tear he gives of ineffectual love.

And while her pure fuperior faith he owns,
Spurns the falfe heart of man and monarchs' crum-
  bling thrones.

VI.

" We too," they cry " a realm could fway ;
  " Lo ! the fceptre, lo ! the rod :
" We too in perilous difmay
  " The edge of battle trod.
" But net to all doth Heaven allow
  " Fate's impetuous tide to ftem ;
" From the haughty monarch's brow
  " Falls the beaming diadem :
" Proud potentates are taught to know
  " The ftrong dominion of tranfcendent woe ;
" When Juftice in her defolating hour
" Subverts the high-built mound and glittering
  " arch of pow'r.

VII.

" Arrang'd by Superftition's hand,

" Mark thefe fragments vaft and rude,

" Which in dread diforder ftand

" To awe the folitude :

" This dreary mafs, tho' fummer fmile,

" Quickening verdure never decks ;

" Circling years the dufky pile

" With defolation vex :

" So power, by fhallow craft defign'd,

" To curb with terrors, not to blefs mankind,

" In barren grandeur rears its naked form

" To the keen lightning's bolt and Heav'n's aveng-

" ing ftorm.

VIII.

" Of harfh misfortune's chaftening pow'r

" Then own the bleft controul ;

" And learn in forrow's wholefome hour

" To harmonize the foul [10] :

" For if when Heaven to triumph guide,

   " Pleasure's maddening rites you seek,

" And, elate with prosperous pride,

   " Scorn the good, and crush the meek " ;

" If groveling in each sensual aim

" You quench aspiring virtue's patriot flame,

" Thy baleful sway what scourging woes attend,

" Than exile days more sad, or e'en thy father's end!

IX.

" To foes a needy suppliant fly,

   " Thy people's love disown ;

" While shame and griping penury

   " Besiege a sovereign's throne :

" Thy revels o'er, thy pleasures fled,

   " Where's a friend thine eye to close ?

" Hateful bigots round thy bed

   " Crowd, and break the last repose :

" No brother's tear is seen to flow ;

" Thy mangled relics an unseemly shew

" Of funeral pomp the tardy mockery wait [12],

" While humbler mortals figh, and tremble to be

" great."

NOTES

ON

THE VISION OF STONEHENGE.

NOTE 1, Page 87.

HAROLD, killed at the battle of Haſtings.

NOTE 2, Page 87.

William Rufus, ſlain by Sir W. Tyrrel in the New Foreſt.

NOTE 3, Page 87.

Richard the Firſt, killed by Gourdon before the caſtle of Chalees, near Limoges.

NOTE 4, Page 87.

Edward the Second, born in the caſtle of Car-narvon, dethroned by Iſabella, and killed by order of Mortimer in Berkely caſtle.

NOTE 5, Page 87.

Richard the Second, depoſed and ſtarved to death.

NOTE 6, Page 88.

Henry the Sixth, killed after the battle of Tewkeſbury.

NOTE 7, Page 88.

Edward the Fifth, put to death by the Duke of Glo'ſter his uncle.

NOTE 8, Page 88.

Richard the Third, killed at the battle of Boſworth.

NOTE 9, Page 88.

See Lord Strafford's fpeech in the State Trials.

NOTE 10, Page 90.

Veræ numerofque modofque edifcere vitæ.

HORAT.

NOTE 11, Page 91.

Allufions to the exile of Clarendon and the death of Lord Ruffel.

NOTE 12, Page 92.

See an affecting account of the death of Charles II. in Harris's Life of that prince.

Published as the Act directs by T. Cadell, Strand, Feb. 1 1711.

MARY

QUEEN OF SCOTS:

AN ODE.

O tu donna, che vai,
Di gioventute, e di bellezze altera,
E di tua vita il termine non fai!

PETRARCHA, Trionfo della Morte.

ARGUMENT.

The Queen, after paffing the night in fight of the coaft of France, which fuggefted to her many pleafing and melancholy reflections, fees the Spirit of the Ifles, who comes from **the** Orkneys furrounded by Ghofts, and announces the unfortunate **voyage** which fhe has undertaken. He foretels the ungenerous **conduct** of Queen Elizabeth, and of her own fubject and relation the Earl of Murray; declares the cruel reception fhe is to meet with from the Reformers; but exhorts her no longer to regret the kingdom of France, where fo many fcenes of horror are to be exhibited in the civil wars of that people, and the maffacre of the Hugonots. He proceeds to predict her extravagant affection for Lord Darnley; her fudden averfion to him; the influence of Rizzio, and the extraordinary end of **that** unfortunate favourite. Her fubfequent misfortunes are then opened; the murder of her hufband; the criminal elevation of Bothwell, and his calamitous death. The cataftrophe of the Queen herfelf is then foretold, and the fate of her pofterity; the peaceful but ignominious government of her **fon;** the civil wars which overturned the throne under Charles the Firft; the fhort-lived joy of the nation upon the Reftoration; the abdication of James; the brilliant reigns of Mary and Anne, which were difquieted, however, by the factions, and embittered by the mifery, of their exiled family; and, laftly, the extinction of the Houfe of Stuart.

MARY

QUEEN OF SCOTS:

AN ODE.

I. 1.

" FAREWELL, dear land¹! thou gallant feat

  " Of courtefy and foft delight ;

  " Thy pleafure-breathing plains retreat,

    " And fink for ever from my fight :

  " Ah ! happy realms, where late I fhone

  " In fcepter'd ftate, in beauty's higheft noon ;

  " When Hymen deck'd his youthful bow'rs,

" And fancy, ever-new, awak'd the laughing hours."

Thus mourn'd the Queen, what time to Gallia's coaft

  She heav'd reluctant many a parting figh ;

And faw, 'midft fears and anxious bodings toft,

  The white cliffs leffen from her lingering eye :

Through the long night fhe watch'd the glimmering

    fhore,

And heard, in doleful trance, the fullen billows roar.

I.   2.

    From Orkney's ftormy fteep

  The Spirit of the Ifles infuriate came,

  Round him flafh'd the arctic flame[2];

His dark cloud fhadow'd the contentious deep[3]:

  Thrice with a whirlwind's ample breath

  He blew the pealing trump of death ;

  While ghoftly legions, fleeting by,

  Swell'd with terrific fcream his dreary cry :

    " Queen of unnumber'd woes ! with evil ftar[4]

  " Borne from each long-lov'd, rapturous fcene away,

    " To realms where everlafting difcords jar,

  " And maddening factions fpurn thy feeble fway :

" What plagues are ripening in the womb of fate,

" A Murray's venom'd guile, a Tudor's deadly

    " hate[5] !

I. 3.

" Nor dance nor feftive air

  " Announce thy dawning reign ;

  " To greet the royal fair [6],

  " A blank relentlefs train

" With funeral vifage frown, and fcoffs uncouth,

" Mocking the frolic fmile of youth [7]:

  " No more with weeping eyes

" Thy hymeneal kingdom wail ;

" Hark ! what anguifh loads the gale,

" What mifts of carnage cloud the reeking fkies [8]!

  " See, on his couch, the lion crouch,

" The heir of Conde's ill-ftarr'd might [9];

  " In wild amaze, his eyeballs blaze—

" Deeds of horror fcare the night :

  " Foul fhepherd, in accurfed mood

" Thy fleeping fold to fmite with murderous rage [10],

" O fhield the hoary warrior's helplefs age,

  " And reverence Montmorenci's blood [11]:

H

" Blot not with endlefs guilt a nation's fame,

" Nor let long ages curfe the deeds they dare not

    " name [12].

II. 1.

" He comes, in beauteous pride array'd,

  " The flow'r of Lennox' ancient race [13];

" On his beaming front difplay'd

  " High valour and majeftic grace :

" He comes, as when the god of day

" Hears on the eaftern hills his proud fteeds neigh

" And chides the lagging hours—thine eye

" Avert, nor truft, fond Queen, the treacherous

    " fympathy :

" Thy heart, that fwells with love's voluptuous tide,

  " Shall mourn the coldnefs of thine altered mate :

" The ftorm of boifterous paffion fhall fubfide,

  " And ardent throbs expire in jealous hate :

" Scar'd pleafure flies from thy unhallow'd bed,

" While vengeance ftalks around, and beckons to

    " the dead.

II. 2.

" What fadly-foothing ftrain,

" What mournful melody hath caught mine ear ?

" Ah! no more the notes I hear—

" The leffening cadence dies along the plain :

" Sweet minftrel, whofe enchanting art

" In ecftafy can lap the heart ;

" Why hath thy mufe advent'rous ftray'd

" From Doria's ftream and Sufa's warbling fhade[14]?

" In clattering hawberk clad, thro' night's ftill

" gloom,

" Stern Ruthven fiercely ftalks with haggard mien ;

" With thundering tone proclaims the victim's

" doom,

" And tears her minion from a doating Queen :

" Thro' the arch'd courts, and ftoried chambers

" high,

" Loud fhrieks of terror ring, and death's expiring

" cry.

II. 3.

" Bid the deep tempeſt roar,

 " And whelm a baleful crew ;

" Proud lord of Inis-tore [15] !

 " Be thine, thy guilt to rue—

" Pent in the dungeon's dark and ſtony womb,

" O'er thee be rais'd a living tomb ;

 " Grim fiends and ſpeƈtres dire

" Hover round thy coward head,

" And ſwart melancholy ſhed

" Her chilling dews that quench th' ethereal fire ;

 " For lo! yon form, that rides the ſtorm,

" Traitor, 'tis thy murder'd king [16]!

 " He joins the hoſts, of monarch ghoſts ;

" Of the days of old they ſing—

 " With ſounds of loud lament they hail

" His ſanguine ſhade, that fires the miſty air ;

" Sublime they float, and o'er the mountains bare

 " In majeſty of midnight ſail : .

" Down heav'n's broad fteep defcend in dread array,

" And in the fhadowy moon's pale confine melt away.

III. 1.

" Ill-fated Queen ! thy ftar, that ftood

    " On the pure zenith's blazing height,

" Now reddening meets the troubled flood,

    " And ftreams with melancholy light :

" In yonder cloud, the book of Fate,

" Read the long fufferings of thy captive ftate ;

" There count the groans, whofe nightly found

" Thrills the wide-water'd moat, and caftle's lonefome

    " round :

" Tho' in thy veins rich ftreams of honour flow,

    " Tho' thy proud hand a double fceptre preft ;

" No genial ties fufpend the ruthlefs blow,

    " Nor love, nor pity melt a rival's breaft :

" ' Perifh the traitor! perifh! ' Shrewfbury cries [17],

" While gentle Melvil [18] veils his forrow-ftreaming eyes.

III. 2.

" Shame to her high-born fon!

" And thou, Britannia, fcorn his abject fway[19]:

" Short gleams of fplendor fleet away,

" And fell rebellion fhakes the fteadfaft throne.

" Uxorious lord [20], thy woes begin ;

" Hear thou the lamentable din

" Of pikes, that ring on Freedom's fhield,

" While Glory pants along the crimfon field.

" With low'ring fcowl a tyrant warrior glares [21],

" Before him kings and wither'd hofts retire ;

" His pale lips quiver with flow-muttering
    " pray'rs,

" His eyeballs gliften with a comet's fire :

" By his fierce breath the imperious deluge driv'n,

" Rolls o'er the ruin'd throne, nor fpares the fhrines
    " of heav'n [22]!

III. 3.

" The waves and wild blasts ceafe,

  " That tore the black profound ;

" In robes of radiant peace,

  " Hyperion flames around,

" And heavenly Mufes ftrike each choral ftring [23] :

" Before the young triumphant king,

  " Flies Joy and towering Fame ;

" But a foul Circeian crew,

" Rufh with blood-ey'd rage to view,

" And hurl to hovering infamy his name.

  " What orb now gleams, with angry beams,

" Through the defert tracts of air [24] ?

  " His courfe half run, the faded fun [25]

" Falls from his refulgent fphere.

  " Twin Queens [26] afcend—though victory

   " breathes

" Immortal pæans round their free-built throne ;

" A father's curfe refounds, a brother's groan,

  " And blafts their inaufpicious wreaths :

" No more—in dark futurity I clofe

" Thy defolated race, and doom of lengthen'd woes.

NOTES

ON

MARY QUEEN OF SCOTS.

NOTE 1, Page 99.

MARY Queen of Scots was married to Francis
the Second, upon whofe death fhe returned to her
own country, in 1561.—Brantôme gives an affecting account of the regret which fhe expreffed on
leaving France:—Ainfi donc qu'elle vouloit com-
mencer à fortir du port; que les rames commençoient
à fe vouloir laiffer mouiller, elle y vit entrer en
pleine mer, & tout à fa vue, s'enfoncer un navire
devant elle, & fe périr, & la plufpart des mariniers
fe noyer, pour n'avoir pas bien pris le courant & le

fond; ce qu'elle voyant, s'ecria incontinent : Ha !
mon Dieu ! quel augure de voyage eſt cecy ! Et la
galere eſtant ſortie du port, & s'eſtant eſlevé un
petit vent frais, on commença, à faire voile & la
chiourme ſe repoſer. Elle ſans ſonger à autre aɛtion,
s'appuye les deux bras ſur la poupe de la galere du
coſté du timon, & ſe mit à fondre en groſſes larmes,
jettant tousjours ces triſtes paroles : Adieu France,
adieu France, les repetant à chaque coup ; & luy
dura cet exercice dolent près de cinq heures,
juſques qu'il commença à faire nuit, & qu'on luy
demanda, ſi elle ne ſe vouloit point oſter de-là, &
ſouper un peu. Alors redoublant ſes pleurs plus
jamais, dit ces mots: c'eſt bien à cette heure, ma
chere France, que je vous perds du tout de veue,
puiſque la nuit obſcure & jalouſe du contentement
de vous voir tant que j'euſſe pû, m'apporte un voile
noir devant les yeux, pour me priver d'un tel bien.
Adieu donc ma chere France, que je perds du tout
de vue: je ne vous verray jamais plus. Elle

voulut fe coucher fans avoir mangé & ne voulut defcendre en bas dans la chambre de la poupe ; mais on luy fit dreffer la traverfe de la galere en-haut de la poupe, & luy dreffa-t-on-là fon liét : & repofant un peu, n'oubliant nullement fes foupirs & larmes, elle commanda au timonnier, fitoft qu'il feroit jour, s'il voyoit & defcouvroit encore le terrein de France, qu'il eveillaft & ne craignift de l'appeller. A quoy la fortune la favorifa ; car le vent s'eftant ceffé, & ayant recours aux rames, on ne fit gueres de chemin cette nuit : fi bien que le jour paroiffant, parut encore le terrein de la France : & n'ayant failly le timonnier au commandement qu'elle luy avoit fait, elle fe leve fur fon liét, & fe mit à contempler la France encor, tant qu'elle peut. Mais la galere s'effloignant, elle s'cloigna fon contentement & ne vit plus fon beau terrain. Adonc redoubla encor fes mots: Adieu la France, cela eft fait, adieu la France ; je peufe ne vous voir jamais plus.—Brantôme, tom. ii. p. 119.

Note 2, Page 100.

It was long thought, in the north of Scotland, that tempefts were occafioned by fpirits, who tranfported themfelves in the whirlwind from one place to another. Thefe apparitions were fuppofed to be feen by the deer, and other animals; and to this day, when beafts ftart, the vulgar imagine that they fee the ghofts of the deceafed.—See Carthon, p. 128.

Note 3, Page 100.

Oppofite to Cape Orcas, the tide runs with remarkable ftrength, which circumftance, according to the iflandic derivation, is fuppofed to have given their name to the Orkneys.—See Campbell's Polit. Survey, vol. i. p. 653.

Note 4, Page 100.

Malâ ducis avi domum. Hor. Lib. i. Od. 15.

NOTE 5, Page 100.

The Earl of Murray and Queen Elizabeth appear, from the hiſtorical evidence which remains, to have been the principal inſtruments of Mary's unfortunate end.

NOTE 6, Page 101.

The reception which the Queen met with in Scotland was not calculated to alleviate her regret.— Nous allaſmes entrer & prendre terre aú Petit-Luc (Petit Leith) ou ſondants les principaux de-là, & de l'Iſlebourg qui n'eſt qu'à une petite liéue de-là, la Reyne y alla à cheval, & ſes dames & ſeigneurs ſur les hacquenées guilledines du pays telles quelles, & harnachées de meſme : donc, ſur tel appareil, la Reyne ſe mit à pleurer, & dire, que c'eſt n'eſtoient pas-là les pompes, les magnificences, ni les ſuperbes montures de la France, dont elle avoit jouy ſi long-temps : mais qu'il falloit prendre patience ; & qui pis eſt, le ſoir, ainſi qu'elle ſe vouloit coucher, eſtant logeè en bas en l'abbaye de l'Iflebourg, qui eft certes un beau baftiment, & ne tient rien du pays, vindrent fous la feneftre cinq ou fix marauts de la ville, luy donner aubade de mefchants violons & petit rebecs, dont il n'y en a faute en ce pays-là ; & fe mirent à chanter pfeaumes, tant mal chantez, et fi mal accordez, que rien plus. He ! quelle mufique, & quel repos pour fa nuit !—Brantôme, tom. ii. p. 122.

Note 7, Page 101.

Randolph, in a letter to Cecil, September 1561, foon after her arrival in Scotland, fhews how harfhly the Queen was reproved by the reformers.— Mr. Knox fays he fpoke on Tuefday to the Queen ; he knocked fo hard on her heart, that he made her to weep as well for anger as for grief. Upon Sunday, 24 September, 1561, her Grace's chaplains in the Chapel Royal would have fung high mafs : the Earl of Argyle and Lord James (i. e.

Murray) fo difturbed the Quire, that fome both priefts and clerks left their places with broken heads and bloody ears. It was a great fport to behold it. Cotton, Lib. Cal. 10, cited in a Hif-tory and Crit. Inquiry into the Evidence produced againft Mary Queen of Scots, p. 174, note.—In what a piteous fituation, continues that ingenious advocate, muft this princefs have been, furrounded with thofe men, who, on the moment of her arrival among them, could, in her own capital, ufe their Sovereign with fuch brutality.

Note 8, Page 101.

Had the Queen continued in France, fhe would have been witnefs to the civil wars of that kingdom, and the maffacre that took place at Paris in 1572.— " Action exécrable," fays Perefixe, " qui n'avoit jamais eu, et n'aura, s'il plait à Dieu, jamais de femblable."—See a particular account of it in De Thou, and Les Memoires de Sully, tom. i. p. 43.

NOTE 9, Page 101.

Gaspard de Coligni, after the death of the Prince of Condé, who was killed in the battle of Jarnac, became the head of the Proteftant party.

NOTE 10, Page 101.

Charles IX. who fired upon his fubjects from the Louvre.—J'ai entendu dire au dernier Marefchal de Teffe, qu'il avait connu dans fa jeuneffe, un vieillard de quatre-vingt ans, lequel avait été page de Charles IX. & lui avait dit plufieurs fois, qu'il avait chargé lui-même la carabine avec laquelle le roi avait tiré fur fes fujets Proteftants la nuit de la St. Barthelemi.—Voltaire, Note à l'Henriade.

NOTE 11, Page 101.

Admiral Coligni was defcended from a fifter of the Conftable Montmorenci.—A curious and circumftantial account of his death is given by

Davila, but the whole narrative affords a very indifferent fpecimen of the humanity of that celebrated hiftorian.————Davila, tom. i. p. 294.

NOTE 12, Page 102.

A deed without a name.   MACBETH.

NOTE 13, Page 102.

See the defcription of Lord Darnly, and the account of Mary's fudden and exceffive affeftion for him, in Dr. Robertfon's Hiftory of Scotland, vol. i. p. 316, 8vo. edit.

NOTE 14, Page 103.

David Rizzio, whofe mufical talents and unfortunate end render him an objeft of pity, was a native of Piedmont. See the defcription of the manner in which he was feized by the Earl of Ruthven, who entered the apartment of the Queen, when fhe was at fupper, in complete armour.

Robertson, Hift. Scot. vol. i. p. 358.—See alfo
a curious letter from the Earl of Bedford to the
Lords of the council of England, giving a particular account of the Death of Rizzio.   Appendix, N° xv.

NOTE 15, Page 104.

The Earl of Bothwell, who engaged the affections
of the Queen after the death of Rizzio, was created
Duke of Orkney, the old name for which is Inis-
tore.—His profperity was of fhort continuance:
being driven from his country, he turned pirate ;
and being fhipwrecked on the coaft of Norway,
was taken and put into prifon there, where he lan-
guifhed ten years, after melancholy and defpair had
deprived him of his fenfes.—Robertfon, Hift. Scot.
vol. i. p. 381.

NOTE 16, Page 104.

There is no room to doubt of Bothwell having
been concerned in the murder of the king, what-

ever an ingenious advocate may advance to make
the guilt of Mary problematical. See Robertfon's
Differtation, in the Appendix to his Hiftory of
Scotland, and an Inquiry into the Evidence produced againft Mary Queen of Scots.—The images
of the following lines are taken from the **popular**
notions of the Scots, relative to ghofts and fuper-
natural appearances; which occur in their old
ballads, and are repeated, even to fatiety, in the
poems afcribed to Offian.

NOTE 17, Page 105.

The Earl of Shrewfbury, one of the lords em-
powered to fee the fentence of the Queen's death
put in execution.

NOTE 18, PAGE 105.

Sir Andrew Melvil, the mafter of her houfe-
hold, whofe affliction at taking leave of her the
Queen reproved with a mixture of magnanimity

and kindnefs.   After a confinement of eighteen years, Mary Queen of Scots had her head fevered from her body, in Fotheringay Caftle, on the 8th of May, 1587.   " No man,   " fays Brantôme, " ever beheld her perfon without admiration and love, or will read her hiftory without forrow."— The defcription of her death has exercifed the eloquence of three mafterly hiftorians, which a reader of tafte will be pleafed to compare, and know how to appreciate.   See the accounts in Hume, Roberfon, and Stuart, and a copy of a curious letter from the Earls of Shrewfbury and Kent, touching the proceedings with regard to the Scottifh Queen, to her Majefty's council.—Appendix to Robertfon's Hift. of Scot. p. 110.

Note 19, Page 106.

James I. of whom it is quaintly, but truly, obferved by Nat. Bacon, " that he fpoke peace abroad, and fung lulla-by at home : yet, like a dead calm

in a hot fpring, treafured up in ftore fad diftempers
againft a back-winter."

Note 20, Page 106.

Charles I. whofe queen Henrietta had a fatal
afcendancy over him.—See Harris's Life of that
King.

Note 21, Page 106.

Oliver Cromwell.

Note 22, Page 106.

The deftruction of the cathedrals and churches
by the puritanical army.

Note 23, Page 107.

The reftoration of Charles II. and the glorious
commencement of his reign, which difappointed
the hopes of the nation—

As a fair morning of the bleſſed ſpring,

　　After a tedious ſtormy night;

Such was the glorious entry of our King,

　　Enriching moiſture dropt on every thing:

Plenty he ſow'd below, and caſt about him light.

COWLEY.

NOTE 24, Page 107.

Εϱημας δι' αιθερος.　　　　　　　PIND.

NOTE 25, Page 107.

The abdication of James II.

NOTE 26, Page 107.

Queen Mary and Queen Ann.

The following Works, printed in an uniform Size with THE MINE, a Poem, and each in a fimilar Manner adorned with Plates, are fold by CADELL, jun. and DAVIES, in the *Strand*.

---

1. THE TRIUMPHS OF TEMPER, a Poem, by WILLIAM HAYLEY, Efq. Eighth Edition. 6s. in boards.

2. ELEGIAC SONNETS, by CHARLOTTE SMITH. Seventh Edition. 6s. in boards.

3. THE PLEASURES OF MEMORY, with fome other Poems, by SAMUEL ROGERS, Efq. Eighth Edition. 6s. in boards.

4. THE PLEASURES OF IMAGINATION, by MARK AKENSIDE, M. D. To which is prefixed, A Critical Effay on the Poem, by Mrs. BARBAULD. 6s. in boards.

5. THE ART OF PRESERVING HEALTH, by JOHN ARMSTRONG, M. D. To which is prefixed, A Critical Effay on the Poem, by Dr. AIKIN. 6s. in boards.

6. THE SPLEEN, and other Poems, by MATTHEW GREEN. With a Prefatory Effay by Dr. AIKIN. 5s. in boards.

7. THE CHACE, a Poem, by WILLIAM SOMER-VILE. To which is prefixed a Critical Effay by Dr. AIKIN. 6s. in boards.

8. THE SHIPWRECK, a Poem, by WILLIAM FALCONER. Ninth Edition. 5s. in boards.